AFTERWARDS
I KNEW
STORIES FROM THE 1ST AND 2ND
WORLD WARS

AFTERWARDS
I KNEW
STORIES FROM THE 1ST AND 2ND
WORLD WARS

Christine Farenhorst

CF4•K

10 9 8 7 6 5 4 3 2 1

© Copyright 2010 Christine Farenhorst

ISBN: 978-1-84550-563-9

Published in 2010
by
Christian Focus Publications,
Geanies House, Fearn, Tain,
Ross-shire, IV20 1TW,
Great Britain

Cover design by Alister MacInnes

Printed and bound by Norhaven AS, Denmark

'Though an army encamp against me,
my heart shall not fear; though war arise against me,
yet I will be confident.
One thing have I asked of the Lord,
that will I seek after;
that I may dwell in the house of the Lord
all the days of my life,
to gaze upon the beauty of the Lord
and to inquire in His temple.'
Psalm 27: 3-4

Dedicated to my dear son-in-law, Scott Wilkinson,
who loves stories of the Great Wars,
and who is a passionate warrior for his Lord
and Saviour himself.

Contents

'But he lingered. So the men seized him and his wife and his two daughters by the hand, the Lord being merciful to him, and they brought him out and set him outside the city.'
Genesis 19:16

THE HOUND
OF HEAVEN

It was quiet and warm in the room and the boy fought against the inevitable sleep that was mastering his small body, falling over him like a wool blanket. Lifting his head from where it was leaning against his grandfather's shoulder, he saw that the old man's eyes were closed. They were sitting in front of a fireplace. The logs were burning steadily. Through the window, in the half-light of dusk, feather-light snowflakes fell from a grey sky. The boy nestled back and sighed contentedly in the crook of the old man's arm. He did not wish this time to pass. He did not wish it to disappear into dreams and ashes on the hearth.

'Tell me a story, Grandfather.'

The old man opened his eyes and shifted the child's position somewhat before he answered slowly.

'I'll recite a poem, child.'

'A poem?'

'Yes, listen carefully. It's long.'

The child was satisfied and closed his eyes as the old man began in a sonorous voice.

I fled Him, down the nights and down the days;

I fled Him, down the arches of the years;

I fled Him, down the labyrinthine ways

Of my own mind and in the mist of tears

I hid from Him, ...

He paused for a moment and the child opened his eyes, worrying out loud with a petulant voice.

'I don't understand the words, Grandfather. Can't you tell me a story instead?'

The old man smiled and put his hand on the boy's cheek.

'A story, child? Always must you have a story?'

The child rubbed his cheek like a cat against the hand. He knew his grandfather would tell him a story. He always did.

'The poem, child ...'

'Oh, Grandfather, not the poem please.'

'Listen, little one. Listen. Or the story you are looking for will disappear.'

And the child closed his eyes again and listened.

The old man continued staring out into the softness of the snow.

'I will explain the poem to you, child. That poem is about someone who is trying to run away from God – about someone who thinks he can live without God. Ah,' and here the old man stroked his beard thoughtfully and smiled to himself, 'but we never can, of course. We never can. If God will have us, then He will have us.'

'The story, Grandfather.'

The child spoke impatiently, while he kept his eyes closed.

'Yes. Yes, the story. Listen, then, for the story is beginning.'

'I fled Him, down the nights and down the days. That is how the story begins. A long time ago ... ah, so long, child, that my beard had not even begun to grow, there was a young man who enlisted in the army. It was a time of war – a time of great war for his country. It was also a very uncertain time and the soldiers in the army were not always sure that they were doing the right thing by fighting. But,' and here he paused reflectively, 'they had to enlist and they had to fight. Because if they did not, their families would be in trouble. They would be put into jail and shot.'

'For not fighting, Grandfather?'

'Yes, child, for not fighting.'

'Why didn't the young man run away? If I don't want ...'

'Hush, child! Hush and listen.'

The child, who had sat up to expostulate his thoughts, leaned back again. The fire crackled and the old man went on.

'The young man was not strong-willed. That is to say, he did not stand up for what was right. Even though he questioned the right of his army to fight, and even though he did not agree with the leader of his country, he still went on to fight. There were others in his country who did stand up – other young men who would not be bullied into conscription.'

'Conscription?'

The child questioned the word sleepily.

'Conscription is compulsory ...'

The old man stopped and then went on, trying to make his words sound simple.

'It's when they make you serve. When the government tells you that you must be part of the army, or navy, or air force. It's when you have to be a soldier.'

'Oh.'

The child said nothing else and for a while there was only the crackle of the fire.

'Then what happened, Grandfather? What happened when they made the man to be a soldier? Was he scared to fight?'

'No. No. It might have been better if he had been scared. But he was not. As a matter of fact, he carried out orders devotedly. His superior officers praised him highly. Perhaps it would have been better if they had not praised him quite so much because he became proud.'

The old man's hands tightened around the child as he spoke and he repeated his last words for emphasis.

'Yes, he became quite proud.'

There was a quiet again and the child sighed.

'What happened then, Grandfather. When the man became proud, I mean.'

The old man slowly began to recite again:

From those strong Feet that followed, followed after.

But with unhurrying chase,

And unperturbéd pace,

Deliberate speed, majestic instance,

They beat – and a Voice beat

More instant than the Feet –

'All things betray thee, who betrayest Me.'

'Grandfather,' the child began again, irritation overruling sleepiness.

'I know. I know,' the old man answered, turning his face toward the fire, 'You don't like poetry. You want the story. I will go on. I will go on with my story.'

He stroked the child's head and continued.

'The man became a storm trooper, a member of the Sturmabteilung ...'

'What's that?'

'The soldiers in the Sturmabteilung were part of the Brown Shirts - especially tough soldiers who went into other people's countries and attacked. They attacked without mercy.'

'Was he mean? Did the man become mean, Grandfather?'

'Yes, I suppose he did. He thought that no one could touch him. He thought that he was in control of everything and he liked that. He knew inside that this was not right, but the feeling of power drowned out the feeling of right and wrong.'

'That wasn't very good, was it, Grandfather? Did his mother not tell him ...'

'His mother had died, child.'

'Oh.'

'But she did tell me ... that is, she told the man, Bible stories when he was a little boy.'

The child sat up and looked at the old man.

'Were you the man, Grandfather?'

'Yes, child. Yes, I was.'

For a while there was no noise. The child sat very still. His eyes were wide open now and his mind groped around for words. He finally phrased a question and it fell softly like the snowflakes against a dark background.

'What happened to you to make you not mean, Grandfather?'

'It was the Hound of heaven, child. The Hound of heaven pursued me.'

'I don't understand.'

'How can you understand. Even I don't understand. But I will tell you what happened.'

The child leaned back again.

'In December of 1941 my army, the German Army, invaded Russia – Russia that big, huge slab of a country. My unit, the men I was fighting with, penetrated as far as the Crimea. The men around me murdered and killed everyone they met – the peasant farmers, the people on the road, anyone ...'

'Did you ... did you kill too, Grandfather?'

'Yes. Yes, I did, child.'

The boy swallowed audibly and then the clock chimed and when it was done the old man continued.

'At some point I was separated from my regiment. We were in a forest and perhaps because of all the bush and all the trees, I became disoriented. All I remember now is that suddenly I was alone. I could hear shots every now and then and I was very much afraid of being captured. After all, we, the German Army, had annihilated so many Russians, so many of them. I thought that if I were captured I would be shown no mercy. And rightly so. Rightly so.'

The fire sizzled as the dampness of one of the logs dropped some moistness into the flames.

'I wandered through the forest for hours and hours. It was very cold and I had no feeling left in my feet. Perhaps, I remember thinking, perhaps I will not die from a Russian bullet wound but from the Russian cold. It became dark, and my heart felt dark and I was afraid not only of death but of what lay beyond death. Then I saw a light shining between the trees – a light not too far away. My eyes riveted onto that light and my feet, numb though they were, walked in its direction. *If the people who live by that light*, I vaguely thought, *if they will not let me in, then so be it. I will not have lost anything. And if they do let me in, well then so be it also.* After what seemed like an eternity, I reached the source of the light. It was a small, wooden cottage. I knocked once and waited warily for someone to answer the door. And someone did.'

He was quiet for a moment.

'Who did, Grandfather? Who answered the door? Was it the dog, the hound of ... of heaven?

Impatiently and wide awake now, the child pulled at the old man's jacket sleeve.

'An old woman answered.'

The old man took up his tale again.

'I saw that she was very old and immediately lost some of my fear. Pushing her aside, I walked in. She lived alone. I could see that straightway. There was no sign of anyone else being there. Perhaps her husband or sons had been killed. Perhaps she had no family. I still do not know that. What I do know is that she was not hostile. She was not angry with me, a German soldier. She looked at me with pity, with compassion. Pointing to the wood stove, she motioned for me to take off my outer clothing.

After I had done so, she took out a towel, knelt down and began to rub my almost frozen feet. Then she gave me some hot tea and some bread. We could not speak to one another because she knew no German and I could not speak Russian. Then she offered me her bed while she slept in a chair by the fire that night.

For three days and nights she cared for me as if she were ... as if she were my mother. I could not understand it. She must have known that I was an enemy soldier. My uniform was obviously German. She must have known also that her people were being slaughtered on every side by the Germans. And she must have known that if the Russian army caught her harbouring a German, she would be shot alongside me. Why, I asked myself a thousand times, why was she showing me such love. Why was she doing this for me?

At the end of the three days, before I left, I managed to ask her this through sign language and through gestures. She smiled. She only had a few teeth, but her love and care truly made her beautiful. Turning away from me, she pointed to a crucifix above her bed.

'I escaped through the Russian lines and made it back to Germany. Physically and mentally it was not possible for me to rejoin the army. Something inside me had changed. It was as if I had, after all, been captured. But not by the Russians. No, not by the Russians. I had dreams, vivid dreams, of people I had killed. I could not eat and every time I closed my eyes there were pictures – terrible pictures of the past.'

The child plucked at his sleeve.

'I do not think that I like this story anymore, Grandfather.'

The old man stroked the child's head.

'Better you live this story through me, than live it yourself, child. Hear it out, and grow.'

The child settled back into the crook of his grandfather's arm.

'Finally I could bear my heavy thoughts no longer and I visited a pastor – a man I had once seen beaten for harbouring Jews. I asked if I might speak with him. He looked at me strangely. He did not trust me and rightly so. But he consented to see me. When I told him what had happened to me, he was silent for a long time. Then he asked me what it was that I wanted him to do. I shrugged and looked down at the floor.

'I am not loved,' I said, 'and I do not love myself. I am sorry for what I have done and would, before God, that I could live my life again. But I know that I cannot. But as it is, I cannot live the way I am either. Ah, I don't know why I came or what I want you to do. I only know that I despise myself and I know that there is no hope for such as myself. When the old woman pointed at the cross, something awoke within me. It has not let me go and it will not let me go. It torments me to think, to look, and I know not what to look for.'

The pastor was quiet and then touched my eyes.

'Perhaps,' he said slowly, 'perhaps the Crimea was your Damascus and I am your Ananias.'[1]

'At the time I did not understand what he meant though I understand it now. I stayed with him for a few months and in that time he opened the Scriptures for me and prayed with me. And I stopped running. The Hound had me.'

The child snuggled against his grandfather. He yawned broadly, closed his eyes and sighed.

'Rise, clasp My hand, and come!'

Halts by me that footfall:

Is my gloom, after all,

Shade of His hand, outstretched caressingly?

'Ah, fondest, blindest, weakest,

I am He Whom thou seekest!

Thou dravest[2] love from Me, who dravest thee.'

The old man was quiet after reciting the last part of the poem. The fire still burned and small flames, like tongues of fire, danced on the uppermost log casting shadows on the walls about the room. Red-hot embers glowed beneath and the child was asleep.

---

[1] This refers to the apostle Paul and his experience on the Road to Damascus. This story can be found in the Acts of the Apostles chapter 9.

[2] Drave is the archaic form and past tense of drive. It means, in this case, compel by force or compulsion.

'For I know that my Redeemer lives,
and at the last he will stand upon the earth.
And after my skin has been thus destroyed, yet in my
flesh I shall see God, whom I shall see for myself,
and my eyes shall behold, and not another.
My heart faints within me!'
Job 19:25-27

The Child

It is quite certain now that the Queen is back in Holland, back on the throne, as they say. Everyone speaks of it. People clump about in groups at the road, talking and grinning, and in the stores they openly share this news. Even the minister, flamboyant on his pulpit last Sunday, thanked God for it. It is good, everyone says, to have her back at the helm. I am glad as well. But I am more thankful for another thing; indeed, I am overwhelmed with the knowledge that the King is on the throne. But let me begin my story at the beginning, at the very beginning a long time ago, when I was little and a child in my mother's arms and Maria was a child in her mother's arms.

I am the daughter of a farmer, a fairly well-to-do farmer, in one of the northern provinces of Holland. Maria was the daughter of an accountant. We were the same age, Maria and I, born on the same day and in the same year, 1918. But that's where the similarities ended. Maria had a dark complexion, curly blue-black hair and was a dainty child. I was fair, had blond straight hair and was a rather plump baby.

My mother died in 1919 of the Spanish Influenza and an aunt, my mother's sister, came to look after our household. I had neither brothers nor sisters. Aunt Freda, a replica version of my mother if I can trust the daguerreotype[3] picture I have of her, was very diligent. She worked around the farm with

---

[3] A daguerreotype is an early photographic process, developed by Jacques Daguerre, in which the image is formed by a combination of mercury and silver called amalgam. The actual image produced is delicate and will be damaged if it is rubbed with the fingers. Daguerreotypes had to be mounted in airtight cases with a glass cover to prevent oxidation from the air and finger marks.

passion for many hours each day, but she was a woman of but a few words. Her affection for me seemed to consist in resolutely scrubbing my face each morning and night, in making sure my ears and nails were clean and in braiding my hair so tightly that my scalp tingled. My father was a quiet man as well, almost to the point of sombre, and I suppose that is why Maria's household held so much attraction for me. But let me first tell you how I met Maria.

The Bettelsteins lived in a small house on our property — a house my father rented out. Emil Bettelstein, Maria's father, was a hard worker. But he didn't just work hard. He also often sang while he worked. Maria's mother, Essie, was likewise gifted with a cheerful nature. They had no other children besides Maria.

It all began one day in May when I was about four years old. I think it was in May because I associate the sweet smell of hyacinths with this memory. Bored with not being able to touch or do things, I walked out of the kitchen into our broad front farmyard. Aunt Freda was spring cleaning, something my father once said with an uncharacteristic twinkle in his eye, she managed to do every season. Undecided about where to go, I dragged my rag doll behind me towards the road. At the road I turned right and aimlessly ambled on, dust kicking up under my small feet.

I remember a distinct feeling of freedom as I looked back over my shoulder at the dwindling farmhouse and I began to hum. For a while I amused myself by throwing pebbles into the rather large ditch at my right side as I walked along. Every now and then a frog jumped up out of the water making me laugh uproariously. After a bit though, this pastime became too commonplace and no longer satisfied my sense of adventure. I worked my way through the roadside grass and stood close to the edge of the water. The fresh smell of growing things and the murky smell of duckweed mingled, pricking my nose. Bright yellow buttercups swayed close to the water. They called out to me and I reached for them. But as I did so, I dropped Emmie, my doll, into the ditch. Horrified I saw the knit one, purl one, blue dress, painstakingly knitted by Aunt Freda, slowly sop up dank water.

Strangely enough Emmie sank standing upright until only the top of her wool head was showing with her two button eyes blankly staring at a lily pad. Without thinking I put my right foot into the water, shoe and all. After all, Emmie had comforted me often enough when I had quietly cried under my blanket at night over some minor disaster. The ditch was not deep but the bottom was slimy and sucked at my shoe. I think I whimpered but am not sure any more.

'You should get a stick.'

The voice startled me and in a rapid swirling motion, I lifted my foot out of the water back onto the land. A little girl peered out at me from the wheat field on the other side of the ditch. For a moment I forgot my doll. I rarely saw other children.

'Who are you?'

'Maria,' she answered promptly and added, for clarification, 'Maria Bettelstein.'

I stared at her and she smiled at me. It was such a sudden, wholly sweet and giving smile that I think it was then that I instantly began to love Maria like the sister I had never had.

'I'll get you a stick,' she volunteered and disappeared between the stalks of grain, reappearing moments later with a sizeable piece of wood. She began to dabble in the ditch-water with it, carefully reaching for Emmie, but only succeeding in pushing the doll completely under water. I put my foot back in, holding onto a clutch of grass for support. Companionably Maria moved as close as she could to the water's edge on the other side. My left foot followed my right and soon I stood, knee-deep, in stinky water. Carefully I bent over, reaching for

Emmie's head but as I did so I slipped and fell face down. An instant later something yanked hard at my braids. Maria had also stepped into the water and she pulled me like a fish on a line towards the shore. I howled and the next minute lay on the grass, gasping and crying at the same time.

'You almost drownded.'

Solicitously, Maria patted me on the back.

'My doll,' I wailed, rubbing my eyes.

'I saved your doll too.'

Emmie, none the worse for the experience was lying next to me between the buttercups I had coveted. I stopped crying and considered how different this day was from other days. Sitting up and reaching for the doll, I grinned at Maria. She grinned back. Wet up to her knees, she did not seem overly bothered.

'Do you want to come to my house?'

I nodded and she reached for my hand. Standing up, I took it and went with her, a wet fish traipsing down through row upon row of wheat.

Some three hundred feet or so from where we had met, the ditch turned sharply to the right. A small wooden bridge led to an old and crooked cottage. The straw roof was a trifle dilapidated but the growing ivy around the windows made it seem friendly and, somehow, as if it were waiting for me. The back door through which Maria took me in, didn't shut properly. Mrs. Bettelstein, a larger version of Maria, was in the kitchen and clucked her tongue when she saw us dripping ditch-water onto the carpet. Without saying a word she began to peel off my clothes. I didn't protest, even when I stood, a moment later, stark-naked on her kitchen table. Maria didn't need any help and had taken off her shoes and stockings by the time Mrs. Bettelstein was vigorously drying me with a towel.

'Get one of your dresses, Maria.'

I sneezed and Mrs. Bettelstein continued her rubdown until my whole body glowed. Afterwards neatly dressed in one of Maria's frocks, she put me in an old chair by the round, pot-bellied stove in the corner. Mr. Bettelstein, a balding middle-aged man with a big smile, peered into the kitchen. His office was in the front half of the house. He laughed when he saw me decked out in his daughter's clothes.

'Well, well,' he said to his wife, 'is this one of the neighbourhood's lost sheep? Have you come,' he added for my personal benefit, 'to stay here then and be another daughter?'

I nodded and volunteered my name.

'I'm Cora,' I said, 'Cora Smink.'

He winked at me and I smiled. I liked all the attention just fine and revelled in the warmth of the stove and the hot tea Mrs. Bettelstein had just poured into a cup. Never mind that the cup was chipped and that there was no sugar. Mrs. Bettelstein's touch, Mr. Bettelstein's wink and Maria's friendship were better than any sugar. Emmie had been propped up by a chair leg and looked none the worse for her encounter with the river. My toes wiggled just for the joy of being alive and cosseted.

Later, after I had been brought home by Emil Bettelstein, and soundly spanked by Aunt Freda for running away from home, I reflected that it had been worth it. Maria had whispered that she would come and visit soon and the taste of the small cottage was sweet on the tongue of my heart.

We became good friends. Not close to town, neither one of us had others with whom to play. We fished together, got lost together, sang together and talked together.

'Why do your mother and father sometimes talk funny?'

'That's Yiddish. It's our language.'

'We just speak Dutch.'

Maria nodded but didn't comment. I explored further.

'Do they speak Yiddish because they come from Germany?'

'No, they speak Yiddish because they are Jewish.'

'Oh.'

My father never went to church and my aunt only attended occasionally. I vaguely knew there was such a book as the Bible, but the whole Jewish race was an enigma to me.

'Why did they move to Holland?'

'Well,' Maria thoughtfully chewed a piece of grass and looked out over the fields.

We were sitting beneath the trees of our apple orchard and the tart smell of ripe apples was all around us.

'Well,' she repeated slowly, 'my grandmother and my grandfather are still in Germany. They live in Dinslaken.'

She pronounced the city's name slowly and painstakingly. I was fascinated. In the first place I had no living grandparents and in the second place it seemed very exciting to have relatives in another country. I forgot my initial question as to why her parents had moved to Holland and just repeated the city's name carefully. We were six now and about to go to school for the first time that fall.

It was during that initial school year that I was allowed to sleep over at Maria's house for the first time. We were both very excited and giggled a lot in class. The teacher, Mrs. Veneman, almost punished us by making us stay after class. But seeing our earnest, repentant faces, she relented and let us go with a reprimand. We ran to the cottage like calves let out to pasture for the first time. We were to sleep in the little attic space under the straw roof. Maria usually slept in a small bedroom of her own, but we had begged and begged that we might make a bed up in the loft. In the end Essie Bettelstein gave in. She often gave in when we begged her for things — things such as stories, an extra cookie or a special meal.

I clearly remember that Essie told us about her childhood that evening, about growing up on the fringe of the Ruhr Valley.

'Our house had gables,' she told us, 'much like the Dutch houses here in the village. We had lots of paintings hanging on the wall. Rembrandt, van Gogh, and others. They were only copies, mind you, but they were still beautiful. My father loved art. And in our attic, not like this little attic, we had bags stuffed full with raisins, currants and sugar, as well as sacks of grain. There was a hook just outside the house, where the attic shutters were. It was lowered by a rope and then the sacks of grain were attached to it and we'd see them swing up and up until they disappeared through the open shutters.'

We both listened, fascinated.

'My father was a rabbi, a man of great importance, the only one in our family who had a secondary education. He was also the cantor in the Jewish community.

'What is a cantor?'

Maria and I asked the question simultaneously as we sat at Essie's feet.

'A man who sings in the synagogue,' she answered softly.

'What is the synagogue?'

This time I was the only one asking the question.

'I know,' Maria said.

'It's a church, a Jewish church,' Mrs. Bettelstein answered, without giving Maria a chance to give me the benefit of her knowledge.

'There's no synagogue in our village,' I said, and then reconsidered that perhaps I wouldn't know, adding, 'Is there?'

'No, there isn't.'

The conversation lagged after that. Mrs. Bettelstein seemed talked out but, wanting to prolong the cosy time by the stove, I asked another question.

'Do you miss going to synagogue and do you miss your mother and father?'

'Yes, I miss my father and mother.'

'My mother is dead,' I volunteered just to keep the conversation going, even though I knew that both Maria and her mother knew.

Mrs. Bettelstein stroked my blond hair and much to my satisfaction, kept talking.

'My father was a good man. He often played with me and with my brothers and sisters. There were ten of us, you know.'

I gasped, not able to imagine life at home with so many brothers and sisters. It would be like having school at home. Mrs. Bettelstein laughed.

'It was really not that unusual, Cora. There were lots of big families on our street. Our mealtimes were noisy, but even with so many there was always enough to eat. I remember,' she went on, 'that often my grandfather invited people off the street to dinner and still there was enough. I also remember that at Passover my father's father, my grandfather, sat at the head of the table in his kittel and talit.'

Glancing at her face and about to ask what a kittel and talit were, I thought the better of it. This was not a time to interrupt. Mrs. Bettelstein was back home — she was a little girl again.

'I asked my father,' she said softly, 'why my grandfather was wearing his white robe and prayer shawl, and my father whispered that Passover was an important occasion. He told me that grandfather always wore his kittel and talit for important occasions. I was shocked because, you see, I knew that the kittel was the robe in which Jewish men were buried.'

It was quiet for a moment before she continued.

'My grandfather was buried in that robe before the year was out.'

Maria and I looked at each other. I could, with some imagination, see a large house in a place called Dinslaken and a long table in a bright room with a great throng of happy people eating and talking together. It was a scene wholly unlike the quiet meals we had at home where my father was up and gone again before I knew it and where Aunt Freda's only noise would be a sigh or a cough or a question pertaining to a cow.

'Whatever made you leave Dinslaken?'

It was perhaps a rude and a personal question, but I was too young to realize it. Mrs. Bettelstein looked at me as if she did not see me.

'I married a Jewish Christian,' she answered, 'I married Emil.'

'Are Jews not Christians?' I responded, surprised.

'Not all of them,' she said, and then, rather firmly 'and now it's time for bed.'

Mr. Bettelstein always read the Bible after supper. I had been to supper lots of times and was familiar with this part of the household routine. But now before tucking us in, Mrs. Bettelstein asked Maria to say her prayers. This was new to me and I listened intently as Maria asked God to take care of her grandparents, her parents and myself and herself, and to forgive her all her sins.

'What sins did you do today?' I asked her later in the dark as we snuggled under the blankets. 'Oh,' she yawned sleepily, 'I don't know. Probably lots.'

I puzzled over this long after she was asleep.

We went through the lower and the higher grades together. We studied languages, algebra and grammar. I won skating competitions and Maria won competitions in poetry recitation.

We became young ladies. That is to say, we thought we were becoming young ladies. Seventeen years old is really only the bottom rung in the ladder of wisdom. But Maria was undoubtedly more mature than I was and I tagged along in her steps. I know that now but did not know it then.

I was over at the Bettelsteins often — now for supper, now for a sleep-over and often for the weekly church attendance in the village. The going along to church had begun when I was eleven. I think it began because I envied the closeness of Maria's family and thought in this way to garner for myself whatever it was that made them so fond of one another. Not that they did not share their love with me. They did. The truth was that once in church, I soaked up all the singing, reading and preaching like a dry sponge.

My father and aunt never made any objections. I loved them too but they were in a different world and not interested in the Bettelsteins' religion, as they called Christianity. It was odd really that they referred to Christianity as the Bettelsteins' religion, but perhaps, Abraham being whom he was, it was not so odd.

'Do you believe in God?' I once asked my father point-blank while we were milking.

'Sure,' he answered calmly and went right on squirting the milk into the pail.

'Well,' I said, 'why don't you go to church then?'

'I worship here,' he said, and the metallic sound of the liquid foaming into the pail punctuated his small sentence with exclamation marks.

'But you never pray,' I said softly, 'and God wants us to pray to Him, doesn't He?'

'Life is prayer,' he said, 'I lead a good life. I don't harm anyone and I take care of my animals.'

It was true. He did those things. He was a fine father too in many ways even if he didn't say much. I never wanted for clothes or for food nor did he stop me as I went on to the higher grades. Many of the girls from surrounding farms were taken out of school after sixth grade and had to help out at home. I actually think that he was quite proud of me even though he never put it into words.

It was in 1938 that Maria's grandparents suddenly showed up one day from Germany. I say 'suddenly' but I'm quite sure it was no surprise to Mr. and Mrs. Bettelstein. There were dark rumours about what was going on in Germany, but no one from the village put too much stock in these rumours. After all, no one in the village was Jewish. Maria moved up to the loft and her grandparents got her room. She did not seem to mind. I offered, after speaking to father and Aunt Freda, to have her come and stay with us, but she hugged me and said that it was very kind but she did not want to leave home.

Mr. Rosen, Mrs. Bettelstein's father, was a rather rotund, old man with a great, white, flowing beard. He wore thin glasses on the edge of his nose and appeared to me to be always weighing situations. I'm sure that he did not like me much as his blue eyes filled with distrust whenever I came. Mrs. Rosen was a thin, small woman not at all like her black-haired, beautiful daughter and granddaughter. She bustled about the kitchen, doing this and that, but really not doing anything. Mr. and Mrs. Rosen did not speak Dutch and often I was left in the dark as long conversations went on and on, conversations in which they would dart quick glances at me every now and then. They only stayed for a month or two. One day I came to find the house rather subdued and later learned from Maria that her grandparents had travelled on to one of the bigger cities, to another contact point. They were headed for Palestine.

The same week in which Mr. and Mrs. Rosen left, two other visitors arrived — two Jewish refugees. Also from the Ruhr district, they had received the address from one of Maria's uncles. Hans Uhr was a distant cousin and Josef Haumann, his friend. Hans was thin and wiry and looked as if he might be the curator of some ancient museum. In stark contrast, Josef was strong and muscular. I whispered to Maria that she had better watch out or he would fall through the roof of the loft into her bedroom. She blushed and laughed and then we both laughed until Mrs. Bettelstein gave us a stern look.

Hans and Josef spoke a fair amount of Dutch. Hans had worked for old Mr. Rosen and was also on his way to Israel. Josef was an orphan and undecided about whether to go on to Israel or to join some kind of underground Jewish resistance movement. He had also worked for the Rosens but had no connections with the family besides that of employee. The four of us, Hans, Josef, Maria and myself, walked out on the path behind the house one evening a few days after their arrival — the same path on which Maria had taken me the first time I met her. It was the end of November and a chill wind blew. I walked in the front with Josef beside me and Maria and Hans followed behind. We were quiet at first but then curiosity overcame my inhibition.

'What are things really like in Germany?' I asked, 'And what made you leave your homeland to come here?'

Initially the boys made no response but then Josef began to talk. Haltingly at first and every now and then lapsing into German, he said that he had, in spite of his twenty-one years, still lived at the orphanage in Dinslaken.

'Two weeks ago,' he recounted in a rich baritone heavy with guttural accent, 'the SA came to the orphanage and forced everyone, little children and babies in arms, onto the street.'

'The SA?' I said, and promptly tripped over a root.

Josef caught my arm.

'Sorry,' I mumbled but it was as if he didn't notice the help he had given me.

'The Sturmabteilung - guards, soldiers. They smashed everything in the orphanage. It was terrible. They ripped the curtains. They broke the preserve bottles and threw them at the walls. After they had finished about twenty-five boys from town came in and continued to destroy. Doors were pulled off their hinges, clothes were thrown onto the street and the windows were smashed as well.'

I murmured how awful this all was. Maria was silent but I could feel her tenseness behind me.

'And all the time,' Josef said, his strong voice catching a bit like a sob, 'about a hundred people from Dinslaken looked on. People who had been our neighbours; people we had known our whole lives just stood there and didn't do anything to help us. On the contrary, many of them laughed and mocked us.'

Behind us, Maria coughed into the wind. I thought about turning around and suggested that we go back to the warmth of the pot-bellied stove in the Bettelstein kitchen. But inexplicably enough I found it exhilarating to walk next to Josef even if the things he was talking about were terrible. We kept walking and Josef kept talking.

'The children had to stand in a side alley and watch. Some were crying. It was cold. Then they had to walk in a procession through the streets of Dinslaken to a school. There were some women too. They were not wearing a lot of clothes and the SA laughed at this. One of my teachers, an old man, was hit on his head and he was bleeding. I gave him some water, water I had to carry to him in an envelope. There were no cups.'

'It must have been,' I ventured gingerly, when he stopped his discourse, 'pretty dreadful.'

He laughed. In any case the noise he made sounded like a laugh but it was carried over in the wind like a groan.

'Yes,' he answered, 'it was dreadful. But we also had fun. Remember Hans, how we never said 'Heil Hitler' in school, but always said 'Drei Liter[4]'.'

He half-turned as he spoke and Hans nodded and laughed with him.

'Ja, yes, I remember.'

But Maria did not laugh and softly gave her opinion.

'May God have mercy on all those who, unlike you two, did not get away.'

Josef turned around again.

'Ah, God,' he said, 'Yes, what does He think of all this?'

Hans swore and Maria stopped walking.

'For shame,' she called out, 'for shame, Hans.'

He apologized and after that conversation lagged. It became even colder and I said we should turn back. And so we did.

Hans left three days later. Maria told me he was planning to travel with the same group of people that her grandparents were travelling with to Palestine. It seemed glorious to me to have such a destination but Maria disagreed.

'It's earthly, Cora,' she said, 'and not the Promised Land that so many Jews make it out to be. But,' she added, 'I can

---

[4] Drei Liter - three litres

understand that people want to go there especially if they have suffered much. Yes, I can understand that.'

Moving onto another topic, I mentioned my father's plans. 'Father says that Josef can work for him for a while, if that would suit him.'

'I'll tell him,' she said.

We were at the farmhouse, in the kitchen, darning socks.

'Josef is very good-looking,' I added, and pricked my finger with the needle.

I sucked it and glancing over at Maria was surprised to see that she was flushed. She did not respond to my comment but bent over her darning so as to hide her face.

Josef came a few days later. My father was glad to have him. Plagued by both rheumatism and angina, he had been thinking about taking on a hired hand for some time. For although I helped him in the barn and in the field, I was not a man. Josef was not a farmer but his willingness made up for much. And his cheerfulness and general noisiness lent an aura of happiness to our evenings and to our dinners that had never been there before. Even Aunt Freda smiled over her mashed potatoes, red cabbage and sausage. It was only when we touched upon the subject of Germany that Josef became reticent and so we never broached it again.

Maria came and went to our farmhouse as before. And, several evenings a week, Josef often with me in tow, went to the Bettelstein's. I looked forward to our walks through the dusk and the dark. I also caught myself looking in the mirror several times a day to see if my blond hair was combed just right and for the first time hated the way it fell straight to my shoulders instead of curling romantically about my ears and forehead the way Maria's did. I sucked in my stomach to make myself look thinner and put cream on my hands to soften their roughness. My ablutions did not fail to escape Aunt Freda's eye and I noted, fleetingly, that she regarded me thoughtfully a few times. There was no escaping the fact. I was falling in love.

There is a tenderness, a sweetness about falling in love that makes the most trivial things beautiful. I found the cows, the sky, the pattern on the curtains, and a host of other things extraordinary and wondered why I had never noted their uniqueness before. The wind, the milk squirting into the pails and the sizzle of potatoes being fried in the iron pan, all these sounds were filled with the goodness of living and the goodness of breathing. I never once contemplated the possibility that Josef might not share my feelings. I just revelled in his company and embraced each day with zeal. It was during this time that the minister, Rev. van Koop, came to see me. He had been the village pastor for as long as I could remember and I was very fond of him. Visiting from time to time, he had included me in his congregation since I first began to come to church with the Bettelsteins.

'Coffee, Dominee[5]?'

'Yes, please.'

He was in his sixties and a widower. His housekeeper was a bit of a dour lady and I always pitied Dominee, as she was reputed to be stingy. Generously putting an extra bit of cream and sugar into his cup pleased me, as indeed most things pleased me right now, and I smilingly took my place opposite him at the table.

'Aunt Freda not home?'

'No, she's gone to see a friend in the village, but she'll be back this afternoon.'

'Father out in the barn?'

---

[5] Dominee - pastor

I nodded.

'Good, because it's you I've come to see on a personal matter.'

I coloured. Was he going to say something about Josef living here? Surely that was all right because after all, Aunt Freda and father lived here too.

'It's about time, Cora, that you considered being baptized and doing profession of faith.'

'Profession of faith?'

'Yes,' Dominee answered calmly as he sipped his coffee.

I had no ready answer. It was true that Maria had made profession two years ago and at that time she had urged me to consider the matter as well. But I was not ready. At least that is what I had told her. Perhaps it had been fear and laziness on my part. Being baptized would mean standing in front of the whole congregation and that was a little daunting. Doing profession as well would mean full membership, attending church twice each Sunday without excuse. There was a certain attraction about not being held accountable.

'Well, Cora?'

'I ... I don't know,' I answered, 'I really hadn't thought much about it lately.'

He put down his cup and looked at me quizzically.

'The times are hard, Cora. And,' he added slowly, 'they will become harder. It's good to take a stand now.'

I looked at the cream in its Delfts Blue container and could not bring myself to meet his earnest gaze. What would father say? Actually, I knew that he would not object. He always said that going to church was my business and if it made me happy, well then, that was fine. Aunt Freda wouldn't say much either. As long as I was polite, clean and helped out around the farm, her primary concerns about my well-being were satisfied.

Josef and I walked to the Bettelsteins together that evening.

'The minister was here today'

'Your minister?'

'Yes, the *pfarrer*, the minister.'

That much I remembered from my German anyway. Josef nodded.

'He wants me to be baptized.'

'Ah, yes, baptism. Well, are you going to be baptized?'

'I don't know. What do you think?'

He stood still and turned his body to me.

'Cora, I cannot tell you what I think. You must feel it here, in your heart.'

He pounded his chest and I got red. He saw it and immediately apologized.

'I'm sorry. I think that being part of a group of people who worship the same thing is very important.'

'Are you Jewish? I mean really Jewish like Mr. and Mrs. Rosen? Or are you ...?'

I let the question dangle in the air. He walked on, head down. But I could see a frown had appeared on his forehead.

'I ...' he began, 'I actually don't know what ...'

He stopped for a moment.

'I know that I saw many older Jews who loved money very much. It seemed to me that they only had time for God when it suited them. This I cannot abide ...'

'Then you believe in God?'

He was quiet again. It was snowing and the ground crackled under our feet. An owl flew by, gliding silently above our heads. When Josef spoke again, it was as if he was forcing his words out, they came so slowly.

'I have seen ... many sad things. People dragged from their homes ... children pulled away from their mothers ... old people kicked ...'

I wished that I had not asked him. I looked at the snowflakes falling and felt an inane desire to lift up my face and open my mouth to catch them. But it would not do right now. No, it would not do at all.

'Believe in God? I do not know the purpose of all these things. Surely if there is a God, He must not be as powerful as people think.'

'I believe in God the Father Almighty, Creator of heaven and earth ...'

The words fell out of my mouth. Old Dominee van Koop had made us memorize the Creed a long time ago.

'Perhaps,' Josef said, smiling just ever so slightly, 'perhaps you have not seen many things and so cannot judge whether there is complete truth in this statement.'

I kicked a hard piece of snow and wondered what Maria would say. But this I did know – that she would know what to say. And I also wondered why I seemed inclined to defend something I was not too sure about myself. Or was I? I wished wholeheartedly that I had not brought up the fact that Dominee van Koop had visited. I wished that I had begun to talk about something else, something like skating or farming. We said nothing else until we got to the Bettelsteins'. And then, at the gate, Josef spoke.

'Maria,' he said, 'Maria, she is very good — very pure, you know what I mean? Perhaps you can talk to her?'

I nodded and looked up at him.

'She is also beautiful,' he added softly, 'like an angel.'

Josef worked for my father for almost a half year before he married Maria and stopped working for my father. I had seen his eyes light up when she walked in; I had seen her hands reach for his hands; and I had seen them kissing in the very same place where Maria had once rescued my doll and myself from 'drownding', as she said. Avoiding seeing them together was hard, short of stopping going to the Bettelsteins' altogether. In the long run, that was what I did.

The day Maria had come to the farm to tell me they would be married, I was hateful about it.

'He has no money,' I said, 'and no family.'

She did not respond but only looked at me with her big brown eyes.

'I think you would be wise to wait,' I went on coldly and practically. 'It looks like war and Josef might be conscripted into the army and then you could become a widow in no time.'

She again made no response but tears filled her eyes.

'Are you sure he loves you,' I whispered, 'and that you are the only one? I have heard that some refugees from Germany have wives who have been transported and that ...'

But she did not let me finish. She got up, put on her sweater and walked towards the door. Before pulling down the handle she turned and looked at me once more.

'You were always a good friend, Cora,' she said, her voice shaking just a bit. 'I love you and miss you and pray for you always.'

I said nothing in return but let her go and after that never went to church again. When by chance I had to walk by the Bettelstein cottage a few months later, I saw that it was empty. Father said that they had moved away and he had thought it wiser not to tell me. I bit my lip and turned my face away. In the months that followed I worked harder than I ever had. Father praised me and said there was no need for a new hired hand, I was worth more than three of them. But when the callouses on my hands grated on the linen bed sheets at night, I wept. I wept bitterly.

The next few years I need not really recount. Everyone knows that at four a.m. on 10th May, 1940 the Germans invaded Holland. It was a shock to me and to many others. Even after Austria, Czechoslovakia, Poland, Denmark, and Norway, I hadn't really believed it would happen. Even though I had taunted Maria with the threat of war and widowhood, I hadn't really thought it would actually happen. After all, business went on as usual, the cows ran through the grass with their tails up in the air and the rooster crowed. My father was much affected by it all and his heart, which had been weak for some years, finally gave up. I buried him in the village cemetery in 1942 and continued to farm with the help of some teenage boys from the village.

The war also took its toll on Aunt Freda. Her hands trembled when she set the table and tears often ran down the wrinkled creases of her face as she sat by the stove. She became more talkative too, after father was gone, and would say strange things such as, 'Cora, I think it will snow tonight', even though it was mid-summer and, 'Cora, where is your doll? Where is the little Emmie doll I made for you? You know you can't sleep without it.' The doll had been put away into the attic years ago, but to humour her I had to get it as she would keep on talking about whatever it was she had her mind on. But we managed fine, the two of us. Our farm was in such an out-of-the-way place that we rarely had visitors and the Nazis stationed in the village, after a few inspection calls, left us alone. The minister visited from time to time, but I closed myself off from him and from anyone else who tried to get personal.

'We need places to hide Jews, Cora.'

I shook my head.

'No, Dominee. I've not got ...'

I stopped. I did have the room and could easily make a hiding place. But I didn't want to hide any Jews — I remembered only too clearly the last Jew who had stayed here and it was a hook in my heart, still bleeding and raw. I needed no other Jews to remind me of this hurt.

'You've not got what, Cora?' Dominee asked.

'You're welcome to some potatoes and grain,' I replied. 'Distribute them as you see fit.'

He shook his head and got up. I saw that he had grown very feeble and I longed to take care of him — yet, at the same time, I longed to be comforted myself. But I said nothing. I only let him out the side door and watched him trudge through the snow to an old bicycle which had rope tied around its rims instead of tires.

It is about the last winter, that terrible winter of 1944-45, that I want to tell you. I remember it as if it were yesterday. It was very cold and the day before Christmas. The frost was thick on the windows and I stood by them, restlessly peering round the black-out curtains even though I could see nothing. There was no joy in me. None at all. Leaning my head against the sill, I traced the outline of the thick layers of rime which had formed inside the house. There was a loneliness in me that was greater than ever before and on an impulse I said to Aunt Freda that I was going out for a walk.

'But it's Christmas Eve ... and we're going to have supper soon ... and, there's the curfew ...' she protested rather helplessly.

'Yes, yes, I know,' I answered rather sharply, 'but I'll be back soon.'

For some reason I wanted to walk past the Bettelsteins' old house. I wanted to see that old cottage with its straw roof and the overgrown ivy. It would likely be encased in snow and ice. But that was all right. Aunt Freda watched me put on my coat and shawl and mittens and clucked disapprovingly.

'You'll catch your death,' she said and hopefully fixed her rheumy eyes on my face, thinking I might change my mind.

But now that I had thought of the idea, I could not let it go and in my mind I could see the warm kitchen, the pot-bellied stove and the great big chair in which I had sat after I had fallen into the ditch.

'Don't worry,' I said over my shoulder, as I opened the door, 'I'll be back soon.'

It was dark outside but the stars shone in the sky above. I wasn't worried about the curfew. It was rare that soldiers patrolled our area. And who would be out on Christmas Eve? Well, so I reasoned anyway as I walked towards the cottage. It was very cold and my footsteps crunched the snow. My mittened fingers soon tingled even though I had them buried far within the lined pockets of my coat. I breathed deeply. It felt good to be outside. I had walked this path so often with Maria at my side. My stomach lurched a bit when I thought of her and I could see the little child I had been so long ago, dragging Emmie along the road here behind me. Where was she now, Maria? Hidden away from the Nazis with Josef? It didn't matter though. I would never see them again. Never!

I accelerated my speed and almost slipped on a piece of ice just catching myself before falling. It was here, I remembered, that I had almost fallen when we were out walking with Hans and Josef. It was no good. I could not escape the past. Memories walked with me wherever I went. I could hear Maria's laughter by the bushes over there sailing a paper boat towards the bridge where I had waited as captain of a tollbooth. I could see her blue dress behind that tree where we had often sat playing with our dolls. And now, almost at the front door of the Bettelsteins' cottage I could see her face in the window, waiting for me to come.

I shook myself. My memory was playing tricks on me. Through the window pane, by the bright light of the stars, a little face peered out at me. The frost and ice had not touched the southern exposure of the cottage and the pane, though not completely clear, definitely showed the form of a small head. A little finger seemed to trace the outline of something and now that I was closer I could see a slender neck, a dark head of hair and a white face. There was a faint light in the background. Perhaps it was a candle. I stopped walking. My heart beat irregularly. Who or how ...? I followed the motion of the little finger tracing up and down, up and down. Then resolutely, I walked around the cottage to the back door. It was not locked and easily opened after I had swept away some of the built-up snow around the steps.

There were several candles on the table in the kitchen. And the boy child, for it was a boy child, stood in the doorway between Maria's bedroom and the kitchen. His hair was dark and curly.

'Hello,' I said for lack of better words.

The child simply stared at me. He didn't say anything. By the light of the candles I could see that he was a slender child, approximately four or five years old. That's how old we were, I fleetingly thought. Yes, that's how old we had been, Maria and I, when we first met.

'Were you looking outside?' I asked him.

'Yes.'

His voice was clear, clear as a little bell, with no hint of shyness.

'Were you watching for someone on the path?'

'Yes.'

'For whom,' I queried on, hesitating in my words, 'for whom were you watching.'

'For you,' he promptly replied.

I didn't answer immediately but looked around the kitchen. There wasn't much left in it. Just the pot-bellied stove and the old table in the corner where Mrs. Bettelstein used to peel her potatoes and clean her vegetables. It was on this old table that the candles were now standing.

'Where did you get the candles?'

'They were here,' he said.

He did not move but just stood there as if he was waiting for something.

'Have you been here long?'

'No, just for a little while.'

'I see.'

I cleared my throat, then asked him what his name was.

'Joshua,' he said in that wonderfully clear voice of his.

'That's a nice name,' I answered and he smiled.

For a moment I was back at the ditch with Maria and Emmie and the buttercups. And I could almost feel the sharp tug on my hair when Maria had pulled me out of the water. 'You almost drownded', she had said. I stared at the child and he stared back at me with his big brown eyes.

'Are you ... do you know Maria Bettelstein?' I asked.

'I'm her son,' he said.

I walked over to the candles and stood looking down at them. I suddenly seemed to understand that Maria and Josef had probably brought their child here to hide him from the Gestapo and that they might also be in the area. But would the boy know? And ought I to ask.?

'Will your mother be back for you tonight?' I ventured.

He shook his head.

'What will you do here all by yourself? Surely she didn't leave you all alone here in the cottage on Christmas Eve?

'It's my birthday tomorrow,' he volunteered.

'How old will you be?'

'Five,' he promptly answered and smiled again, adding, 'I think that my mother forgot.'

'Who,' I asked, 'will take care of you?'

'You will,' he said and never let go of me with his eyes.

We walked back to the farmhouse together. He held my hand all the way.

'Were you not afraid by yourself in the cottage?'

'No.'

The answer was simple and direct. He'd had a coat stowed away in the bedroom as well as a backpack of sorts and he carried it like a little soldier. Before we left he'd taken out a lion to show me. Well-worn and much-loved, I could see Maria's touch in the stitches. She had been such a good seamstress.

'What is your name?'

'Cora,' I said, wondering that he should ask, for would not Maria have told him who I was?

He stopped suddenly, in the middle of the path.

'Do you really want me to come with you?' he said, in a still and very small voice, 'Because if you don't ...'

I hastened to reassure him that I did and we walked on. I carried the lion and every now and then he reached up to stroke it.

Aunt Freda was waiting at the door.

'Hello, Cora. I was getting worried. I ...'

She stopped abruptly and stared at Joshua. Joshua stared back and held onto my hand.

'This is Joshua,' I said lamely.

But Aunt Freda, always sedate and particular, smiled and held out her arms, kneeling down to engulf the child in a hug.

'I'm so glad you came,' she said and he smiled at her.

'I like you.'

After the hug he walked right in. His shoes, for he had not had boots, trailed snow into the room. We stood at the doorway and grinned at one another, something, I might add, we have never really done. Like a small king he sat down on the sofa.

'This is nice,' he said and smiled at us both.

'Can we keep him?' Aunt Freda whispered.

He ate well and Aunt Freda at no point questioned me as to where he came from. She seemed enchanted by the fact that there was a child in the house and I even wondered if she perhaps thought it was myself and that time had turned back. When we had eaten our fill of potatoes and carrots and applesauce, I stood up to clear the table. Joshua looked at me with his Maria eyes.

'Well,' I said, 'what is it? Are you still hungry after all? Do you want some more potatoes or apple sauce?'

Aunt Freda already had the serving spoon in the pan ready to scoop out another portion when he answered.

'No, thank you,' he said, 'but aren't you going to read the Bible now?'

'Is that what you're used to?' I asked.

He nodded. Aunt Freda sat down again. She didn't protest but looked at me expectantly as if the child had asked for some after dinner dessert that I had tucked away up my sleeve. We had a Bible. As a matter of fact, Maria and her parents had given it to me for my twelfth birthday. It was in the dresser drawer of my bedroom. I went upstairs to get it and then, because it was after all Christmas Eve, turned to Luke chapter two and read the first twenty verses.

And it came to pass in those days, that there went out a decree from Caesar Augustus that all the world should be taxed ... (KJV)

Aunt Freda sat quietly, her hands folded in her lap and her eyes closed.

And so it was, that while they were there, the days were accomplished that she should be delivered. And she brought forth her firstborn son, and wrapped him in swaddling clothes, and laid him in a manger; because there was no room for them in the inn.

When I was done, I closed the Bible and laid it on the table. Aunt Freda smiled.

'That's a nice story,' she said, 'about a little child.'

I smiled back and again I got up to clear the table but again Joshua eyed me as if there was some unfinished business.

'What is it now, boy?' I said, this time a trifle irritably.

'You've not thanked God yet for the food.'

'Fine,' I said, 'since you seem to be on such good terms with the Lord, you thank Him.'

He smiled and folded his hands. Aunt Freda, after observing him for a moment, did the same and I followed suit.

'Dear Father,' he said in his childish treble, 'we thank you for this food.'

Then he got up and began to help clear the table.

After the dishes Aunt Freda busied herself looking for puzzles, other toys, and my old flannel nightgown.

'He has to have something to sleep in, Cora,' she explained and held up the yellow garment with something akin to pride.

I smiled. It was fine with me.

'Listen!'

Aunt Cora held her finger to her mouth, hushing any reply I might have made. I listened. Joshua was singing. Lying on the couch and hugging his lion, he sang a song. I don't remember the words. Perhaps there were no words. I can only tell you it was beautiful to hear.

The next morning we all went to church. You might think this was foolish. But you see in the first place, I had already thought of an alibi for the child. I would tell people that he had been sent by The Children's Placement Bureau in Amsterdam. Everyone knew that Amsterdam and its population was starving and that children from there were being settled on farms in order to feed them. In the second place, Joshua had asked me if we might go to church and in the third place, it was Christmas.

We were almost late. The sexton was in the process of closing the big, wooden, double doors as we hurried up the church steps. He remembered me and smiled.

'Good morning, Miss Smink. A blessed Christmas to you all.'

Aunt Freda smiled at him. She had been pleased by the ringing of the bell and had expectantly looked up at the sky as we walked the last few blocks in the village to the church. I pushed her along inside. The foyer was empty and I was a bit nervous now that we were finally here. I stood in the doorway to the sanctuary. The aisle seemed long and I squeezed Joshua's hand so hard that he pulled it out of my grasp. A woman in the back pew made a motion with her hand and moved over. There was room next to her and smiling gratefully, I took Joshua's hand into my own again.

Moving into the pew, we sat down. Aunt Freda followed us. And the service began.

It was good to be in church again. I was glad that I had come. Joshua leaned against me and Aunt Freda sat quietly, every now and then looking around at all the people and smiling at anyone who happened to meet her eye. It was a moving sermon and Rev. van Koop had just finished his second point when suddenly the front doors of the church were ripped open and loud footsteps resounded in the foyer. The woman next to me, turned her head and paled.

'Razzia[6],' was all she said to me and my heart sank.

There were about a dozen soldiers in all, I think, and one commanding officer. He was a big, heavy-set man who stalked up the aisle towards the front. The others blocked off the entrance. Joshua sat without moving. I put my arm about his shoulders and felt my legs begin to shake. The officer reached the front of the church. He had something which looked like a whip in his hand and he hit the side of his leg with it. It made a swishing sound and I think it was meant to intimidate us. Rev. van Koop had stopped speaking but at this juncture, he cleared his throat and asked if there was something with which he could help the officer.

'I'm looking for a child,' the officer replied with guttural German accent, 'one Jewish child.'

'A child?' Rev. van Koop said.

'Ja, one child,' the man reiterated, 'and no one will get into trouble if someone tells me where is this child?'

It was deathly quiet in the church. No one spoke and no one moved.

'This child's parents escaped from prison a few days ago and were last seen heading to this area.'

---

[6] Razzia - Dutch word for raid

It was still quiet. I pushed Joshua onto the floor and indicated that he should lay down under the pew. The woman next to me held out her hand towards me and when I, hesitatingly, put my own in it, she gave it a warm squeeze.

'So,' continued the officer, 'if no one speaks, then we wait. Ja?'

He began walking back down the aisle, searching faces, looking at both parents and children as he did so. Rev. van Koop began to continue his sermon but was stopped by the officer who turned around.

'Off the pulpit! Off, I tell you! Go and sit with the people. Not another word or I will shoot you.'

Rev. van Koop silently descended the pulpit steps and sat down with the elders. The officer had by this time almost reached the last pew — the pew where I was sitting with Joshua and Aunt Freda. Aunt Freda had followed the proceeding with great interest.

'A child,' the officer said again, 'one little child. Come now, one of you must know about this child.'

He had reached our pew now and Aunt Freda suddenly stood up.

'I know about a child,' she said.

I could feel Joshua with my feet and tried to control the way my teeth wanted to chatter.

'You know?' The officer stood squarely in front of Aunt Freda and repeated, 'You know where is this child?'

'Yes,' she answered simply, 'I heard about the child ...'

She stopped and put her finger in her mouth, something she frequently did when she was trying to remember something. Then she took it out and went on.

'This child, he was very poor and had no place to go.'

'So where is he? Where did he go?'

The officer's voice rang through the church.

'He was in a barn.'

Here Aunt Freda smiled at the officer. He did not smile back.

'You are making a joke?'

The officer was rapidly losing his temper. Aunt Freda was genuinely confused now.

'A joke?' she repeated a trifle dully, and again, 'A joke?'

The officer struck her face with the palm of his hand and she began to cry. She was not upset I knew, with the pain of the abuse, but because he did not believe her. Whenever I became upset or irritated with her if she went on about something, she could not be placated until she had finished her story.

'I am not joking,' she cried, holding her cheek, 'there was a child. And He was born in a manger. I know it is true and you can ask the shepherds if you don't believe me.'

Something dawned in the officer's face. He looked at me.

'She is your mother?' he asked.

I stood up as well and put my arm around Aunt Freda.

'She is my aunt,' I said softly.

'A half-wit?' he taunted.

'No,' I answered, surprising myself, 'she is not a half-wit and she speaks of a real Child, the Christ-Child. And only those who deny Him are half-wits.'

I looked him full square in the face and beyond his face, at the end of the aisle in the elder's pew, Rev. van Koop smiled at me. I smiled back just before I was hit in the face as well and ordered to accompany him to the front of the church. He harangued the congregation for a full ten minutes, pointing to me from time to time as a bitter example of insubordination before he left again, warning everyone that he would be watching us leave the church and that the penalty for harbouring Jews was death.

As soon as the door closed behind the Gestapo, everyone got up and began to talk. Rev. van Koop edged his way past the people towards me. Both Aunt Freda and I were surrounded by many solicitous people who asked if we were all right, did we want to sit down and wasn't it a miracle how things had gone? By the time we were done with shaking hands and answering questions, a full five or ten minutes had elapsed.

In the end I made my way back to the last pew, worried about how I would smuggle Joshua back to the farm. Or perhaps it would be wiser to ask someone else to take him now. But who could I ask when the search for this child was so intense? Sliding into the pew, I knelt down to look under the bench. There was no one there. I crawled on my hands and knees to look further. There was nothing. Just empty floor no matter which direction I looked. I stood up and in my haste banged my head. It was already sore and I saw stars. Rev. van Koop took my arm.

'He's not here,' I almost wept as I spoke.

'Who's not here?'

'The child,' I said, 'the child I took in with me. The Jewish child ...'

My voice now sank to a whisper, and I continued.

'The child that the officer was looking for and could not find.'

The congregation, by this time, had all gone home. Rev. van Koop and the sexton both helped me look. Outside a brisk wind blew. We never found Joshua that day, nor that following week or month and at length gave up. But after the war I received a postcard.

'Joshua sends greetings, Love, Maria.'

It was post-marked Israel and someday, someday I shall go there and see this Christmas child again.

'When they had finished breakfast,
Jesus said to Simon Peter, "Simon, son of John,
do you love me more than these?" He said to him,
"Yes, Lord; you know that I love you."
He said to him "Feed my lambs."
He said to him a second time,
"Simon, son of John, do you love me?"
He said to him, "Yes, Lord; you know that I love you."
He said to him, "Tend my sheep."
He said to him the third time,
"Simon, son of John, do you love me?"
Peter was grieved because he said to him
the third time, "Do you love me?"
and he said to him,
"Lord, you kow everything; you know that I love you."
Jesus said to him, "Feed my sheep".'
John 21:15-17

Feed my Sheep

We all wait. Some people know they are waiting and others do not know that they are waiting. But always, whether perceived or unperceived, the moment for which we are waiting comes along. It may come as a sharp rap upon the knuckles; it may come in a still, small voice; or it may come in a seemingly impossible situation. But it always comes - and it always results in a confession of the mouth, in an expression of faith, in a moment of truth - with eternal consequences.

The little village of Hartenhand, Holland, lay in a valley, warmly tucked between hills and trees like a treasure in the hand of a child. Small but alive, it had weal as well as woe, love as well as hatred and health as well as sickness. For indeed, no place is exempt from contrast and no place has complete perfection in this life. There are those who believe there is perfection in this life. They may not say so directly and they may disagree violently when the idea is put to them, but they consider their hearts and conditions within the boundaries of God's law - within an area that needs no change. These are legalists, and they also lived in Hartenhand. They forget that God used David - David and five smooth, stones - to kill Goliath.

The main road through the village of Hartenhand, and the only road in the village, lay open and empty at dusk. Peter Straven stood by the window of his study. Shelves upon shelves of books flanked behind him as if they were the vanguard of an army. It was Monday evening and the hour before curfew. Some houses already had their curtains drawn - drawn tightly so that the lamps lit within their living rooms would not with a single faint beam make them liable for arrest in this hour, this fall of 1944.

It had been a difficult, but not insurmountable, time for the people of Hartenhand and for their pastor during the onset of the war. Those first few days when the German troops had crossed the Dutch border had been humiliating, to be sure. Hartenhand was directly located on one of the invasion routes of the German army. Thousands of soldiers had pompously marched through the main street, 'left - right, left - right', as villagers watched anxiously through their first-story windows and from second floor balconies. Whether old or young, war seemed incomprehensible and inconceivable. Although patriotism had run high the last months prior to the invasion, neutrality had been predicted. Holland had been neutral during the First World War and people rationalized that there was no reason why she should not be neutral this time. But the invasion had happened and it was followed hard on the heels with surrender and capitulation. Both events were bitter pills to swallow - yet once they were down life went on.

Hartenhand was a village of age-old solidarity. It had always prided itself on being unified, on being one. There was one butcher shop; there was one grocer; there was one doctor; there was one church; and there was one school. Those who were of the opinion that any of these fell short, were welcome to move to another town. Some did. Peter Straven had been pastor here for the last two years. It was his second congregation.

When Jans, Peter's wife, called him down for supper, he was still standing by the study window. He was somehow oddly dissatisfied with himself. He detected a feeling of smugness within his bones, within his heart. He had, his mind told him, worked hard. His sermons surely went beyond skimming the surface; they might even be termed uplifting. He always prayed for the queen, a matter which took some courage, although the local policeman was decidedly pro-orange. And he religiously listened to the BBC radio broadcasts. (There was a radio hidden in his attic.)

'Peter!'

Jans called, somewhat impatiently, a second time, and his hand reached for the curtain.

'Coming.'

He laboriously pulled the big, brown drapes across the panes and the room became dark. Feeling his way across the study, he stubbed his big toe against a book on the floor. Flicking on the light switch, he picked it up and saw that it was his commentary on the book of Romans.

Supper was eaten in relative peace. There was no abundance of food but the staples of potatoes and brown beans were hearty and satisfying. Kobus, the baby in the highchair was tired, whining every now and then. Seven-year-old Simon was pensive. Leaning his elbows on the table, he stared at the wallpaper.

'Father?'

'What, son?'

Peter answered automatically, his thoughts still busy with usefulness, with doing good. 'Father?'

'Yes, son.'

Peter's voice was a little louder this time and he now looked directly at his oldest.

'You weren't listening the first time.'

The child's voice was petulant.

'I'm listening now.'

'Will all the German soldiers go to hell?'

Jans put down the fork in her hand.

'What kind of question is that Simon Straven? You shouldn't ...'

Peter interrupted his wife.

'It's a good question, Jans.'

She began to protest, but her voice was drowned out by Simon's eager voice.

'We played 'end of the war' today. Nicholas was the mayor, Rolf was the judge, Harry was a German soldier and I was the undertaker.'

Peter cleared his throat, formulating a reply suitable for Simon's age level while playing with the napkin by his plate.

'About hell,' he began, but Simon, clearly excited about his afternoon's work, went on, his enthusiasm uncurbed by the interruption.

'After the judge and the mayor killed Harry, I buried him.'

'How did you ... ?'

The question came simultaneously from both parents and Simon grinned at them.

'I put him in the coal bin. There's no coal in there anyway. But Harry's mother called him for supper and she was angry when he told her he couldn't eat because he was a dead German soldier. She said all German soldiers will go to ... '

'Yes, I know,' Peter finished the sentence for his son, 'to hell.'

'Yes, that's what she said. But Nicholas told her we didn't know that for sure and then she really got angry at him.'

He stopped.

'Eat your beans, Simon.'

Simon took his elbows off the table, picked up his fork and began moving beans around his plate.

'Well, do all the German soldiers go to hell, Father?'

He kept his eyes on his father.

'Who goes to heaven, Simon?'

Peter countered his son's question with one of his own.

Simon's answer was instantaneous.

'The people who believe in Jesus.'

The baby's whining increased and Jans stood up and took him out of the highchair.

'That's right, son.'

Peter smiled approvingly at his firstborn.

'So if ... if a German soldier loves Jesus ... ' Simon hesitatingly began and then paused.

Peter nodded encouragingly.

'That's correct, son.'

And he could not help but remember, in just one split second, how his visit to Arnold Visser had gone last year - a visit to inform Arnold that his son had died.

Tall and thin, formality couched even in his fingertips, Arnold Visser was the local doctor. Although it was after office hours, Arnold had shown no surprise at his pastor's visit. Peter had tripped and fallen over words, many words, about how the Lord gave heavy burdens to some and about how life was a mystery. Arnold had regarded him from behind his desk, folding his delicate surgeon's hands with the clean, short fingernails, interrupting quietly.

'Dominee, why don't you say what you've come to say?'

Peter had swallowed audibly, willing the right words to come. The bottles and jars of medication on the shelves had sat quietly; the rain against the window had pelted as if to penetrate the glass; and Arnold had spoken again before he had found the right words.

'My son loved Jesus, Dominee.'

The shapely hands had loosened their hold on one another and had lain separately, side by side, on the desk.

'He is in heaven. Isn't that what you've come to tell me?'

The doctor's words were clipped and precise as if they were conducting some simple surgery. It was not exactly what Peter had been trying to say. As a matter of fact, he was not sure that Albert Visser was in heaven. Although the youth had been a church member and passionate member of the underground, he had also drunk more than was good for him and profanity had been his second language.

'He is in heaven.'

The doctor stood up as he repeated the words. Peter saw that the hands now gripped the desk and that the knuckles showed white.

'Thank you for coming.'

And Peter had left with the newborn words with which he had been labouring in birth pains, caught in his throat, unborn.

The baby's crying brought Peter back to the present.

'Say goodnight to Papa.'

Jans held the child out to him. He kissed Kobus affectionately and watched his wife carry the baby boy out of the dining room.

'Father ... Father ...'

Simon pulled at Peter's sleeve after Jans had left the room.

'What, son?'

'Why does Harry's mother think all the German soldiers will go to hell? Doesn't she know the part about loving Jesus? She goes to our church, Father, so shouldn't she know?'

Peter lifted his seven-year-old son onto his lap, big as he was.

'Some people forget. They like to think that they are the only ones doing all the right things ...'

'The right things?'

Simon was puzzled.

'Well, things like going to church twice, putting some money into the collection plate, praying before and after meals, reading a chapter in the Bible each day at a set time ...'

'We do all those things.' Simon edged the words in quickly.

'Yes, but you see, son, if your heart isn't in any of these things, it doesn't matter. And if those things make you proud, it doesn't matter. What does matter, and what is the only thing that ultimately matters is our love for the Lord Jesus.'

'So Harry's mother doesn't love the Lord Jesus?'

'Well, no, son, I wouldn't say that. She's been hurt. You know that her husband was arrested. That's why she now really wants to believe that all Germans ...'

His words were rudely interrupted by a sharp knock at the back door.

'Now who ...?'

Peter put Simon down and walked towards the back door. Simon followed hard on his heels.

'Who's there?' Peter spoke softly, warily, before opening the door.

'Henk Ten Wei.'

Peter breathed easier. Henk was a church elder and a friend. Quickly undoing the chain lock, Peter opened the door wide enough for a stocky, middle-aged man to slip through.

'What brings you here, Henk?'

Peter relocked the door as quickly as he had opened it. Henk wasted no time.

'We have a man on our hands who needs a place to stay and ... '

He caught his breath as Simon stepped out from behind his father.

'Hello, Mr. Ten Wei.'

'Hello, Simon.'

Henk looked at Simon doubtfully as he returned the greeting.

'Simon, go up and see if mother needs your help.'

'But she's putting Kobus to bed and she ... '

'Go up, son.'

Simon knew when not to argue and he left, but not before he had turned, saluted and said, 'God save the Queen, and I, Simon Straven, am her loyal subject.'

Both men smiled and Peter invited Henk to walk through and to sit in the dining room. There was a space of silence as Henk stretched his feet under the table. Then, without any small-talk, Henk reiterated his initial sentence.

'As I began to say in the kitchen, there's a man, a Jew, Peter, who needs a place to stay immediately. We've never asked ... '

Peter held up his hand to halt the flow of words engulfing him. His heart urged him to respond unhesitatingly, 'Let the man come here. Of course we'll take him.' But something held him back. And deep within himself he knew that it was fear – the kind of fear that separates faith from works.

'I know,' Henk went on softly, leaning towards Peter, 'that you have a separate attic over two of the bedrooms and that, although van Driel made an almost invisible opening in the ceiling, access is difficult. But we think this man can easily pass as an Aryan, as your relative. He looks remarkably like you. Don't you have a brother in Rotterdam?'

Peter nodded, ill at ease and nervous, well aware of what would be said next. Henk continued.

'Well, as I said, he doesn't appear Jewish. We've already got his papers made up as Arend Straven ...'

'You've already got them made up? But you didn't know ...'

There was anger in Peter's voice, anger coupled with shame. He knew there should not be any hesitation on his part, but he could feel the fear building up within himself. He knew and had always known, that a moment like this might come - a moment in which all his words would be tossed into a Biblical sieve to be measured for sincerity - and that sifted, they might be found wanting.

'I knew,' Henk said, and repeated, 'I knew.'

Peter coughed to hide his emotions before he spoke again.

'Where is he?'

Henk leaned over.

'He'll be brought here shortly. I only just got word myself. It wasn't safe for him to stay on at ... well, never mind where he was. The less you know the better.'

Peter was quiet and stared at the empty food dishes on the table. Henk went on talking, oblivious to the discomfort of his pastor.

'You know, that was an excellent sermon on Romans 10 yesterday. I never thought of my own zeal as the kind of zeal that the Pharisees had ... a zeal that wanted to fulfil the law. But, you made it so clear that we have to depend on grace.'

He drummed his fingers on the tablecloth and slowly chose his next words.

'Perhaps I've been guilty of not thinking enough of my own unworthiness and my total dependence on God's grace.'

Peter did not respond. He only half understood what Henk was saying, even though the man was echoing his last sermon. Henk continued.

'We often live lives within walls of our own making and depend on traditions that we feel comfortable with. Sometimes these traditions stand par with the Bible. You know, I think that legalism is more difficult to fight than the liberalism that is creeping in. We have to be on guard.'

He smiled suddenly and stopped.

'Enough of my philosophizing when there is so little time.'

He stood up, held out his hand and Peter shook it.

'I'll check in with you later this week. Meanwhile, there's no need to worry a great deal. A brother from Rotterdam is no strange thing right now. No one will suspect a thing if he keeps a low profile. We'll find him another address shortly.'

And Henk walked out as quickly as he had come in.

Peter informed Jans about their prospective house guest as soon as she came downstairs and was somewhat shamed by her unstinting and immediate desire to help a fellow human being. Simon was still upstairs changing into his pyjamas. Together they decided not to tell their oldest that the man was Jewish, but simply to say that he was an uncle visiting from Rotterdam and that he needed a place to stay for a while. The boy did not question them.

Peter was uncomfortable with Arend from the beginning. He arrived only an hour or so after Henk's departure. Tall, blond and muscular, and strikingly similar in appearance to Peter, Arend shook hands with the Straven family. Good-naturedly he lifted Simon onto his shoulders.

'You and I are going to get along just fine.'

Simon cheered and exploded into talk about all sorts of things, before he was taken to bed by Jans.

'Would you like some coffee? It's surrogate[7], but it's hot.'

'Yes, thanks.'

Arend had settled down into a big chair next to the pot-bellied stove and smiled at his host. Peter poured him a cup.

'Sorry, there's no sugar.'

'That's all right.'

There was a silence. The clock ticked and outside there was a stillness. Peter imagined that he could hear noises, unsettling noises, and stiffened perceptibly. Arend regarded him thoughtfully while he sipped his coffee.

'You know, I'll only be here a short while. A few days at the most.'

'Yes, I know.' Peter coughed, and felt constrained to go on. 'You're very welcome. We're happy to have you stay with us.'

'You're a minister, aren't you?'

And it seemed to Peter that a world of implication was wrapped around the question.

'Yes, I am,' he replied.

Arend shifted his position in the chair somewhat.

'I'm an atheist.'

He went on sipping the coffee and nonchalantly dangled his feet over the edge of the chair.

'Oh.'

---

[7] Surrogate - real coffee was hard to find during the war due to shortages and rations. Some people improvised and used other products to make coffee substitutes or surrogates.

Myriad thoughts shot through Peter's brain but none of them surfaced to his mouth.

'Does my being an atheist offend you?'

Arend smiled at his host and his fingers embraced the warm cup he held. Peter licked his lips and was about to answer when Jans walked back in.

'Ah, Peter gave you a cup of coffee.'

She sat down and picked up her knitting.

'Where are you from, Arend?'

'I think it would be better if I didn't tell you that. I think you merely have to regard me as a brother and brother-in-law from Rotterdam. As to my occupation, I had a bicycle shop and it was bombed. If I told you more, it might be confusing and besides,' he went on, pointedly looking at Peter, 'I'll only be here for a few days.'

Jans and Simon and even baby Kobus, adapted well to the new house guest. He was full of laughter and stories about people he had met, with an amazing gift of mimicry. Simon, whose teacher was ill with pneumonia and who, consequently, did not have school, hung on to Arend's every word and was full of awe at the push-ups he performed in the living room.

'Can we go for a walk, Uncle Arend?'

It was Arend's third day at the Straven's. Simon wheedled on.

'I'll take you to Mrs. Rutger's next door. She always gives me a peppermint. Well, anyway, a piece of one. They're old and small, but you can make it last a long time if you don't suck and the smell goes up your nose and ...'

'Simon.'

Peter, who had been on his way up to the study, called out to the boy.

'Yes, Father?'

'Can you come up here for a minute?'

The boy's footsteps resounded on the stairs and he was in the study almost before his father.

'Here I am, Father.'

'Son ... ' Peter paused for a moment and then continued. 'Son, it's not wise for Uncle Arend to go outside too much ...'

'Oh, I see.'

The boy was silent for a moment. They had told him that Arend was a refugee and that he needed a place to stay and that it was good for everyone to assume that he was an uncle.

'But Father ...'

'Yes?'

'Well, isn't it more dangerous for him never to go out? Our neighbours have seen him and if he's supposed to be your brother, why would he never go out? Wouldn't they think ...?'

The boy left his question dangling and Peter had to agree with him. A minute later he watched Simon and Arend walk down the main street, hand in hand.

It was while they were gone that Willem Poske, suspected by many to be an NSB[8] agent, called at the parsonage. Jans let him in through the front door.

'What can I do for you, Willem?'

He took off his hat and twisted it about in his hands.

'Oh, nothing in particular, Mevrouw[9] Straven.'

His nasal tones crept into the foyer and up the stairs.

'I had some extra food rations come my way and wondered if you and the Dominee might like to have them.'

---

[8] NSB - Nationaal Socialistische Beweging or National Socialism Party (or Nazi).
[9] Mevrouw - Dutch word for Mrs.

Jans hesitated. She wondered where Willem had obtained them. But food was food, besides which it might be wise not to offend this man.

'Thank you, Willem.'

He smiled ingratiatingly at her.

'Saw that you had an extra house guest.'

'Yes, yes, we do. My husband's brother from Rotterdam. Things are pretty difficult there.'

'Is the Dominee in?'

'He's working on his sermon, Willem.'

'Ah, his sermon.'

'Yes.'

Jans wondered if she could simply ask him to leave.

'I guess,' Willem went on, looking at Jans through narrowed eyes, 'that would be the Lord's Supper sermon for this Sunday that the Dominee's working on.'

'Yes, I suppose.'

Jans was becoming a little impatient. Peter had heard the doorbell and invisibly listened in on the conversation while he stood at the top of the stairs.

'Your brother will be happy to have the fellowship of Lord's Supper here. I'm just allowing ...' Willem went on and repeated, 'I'm just allowing, that the good man is a member of our church.'

'Yes, of course he is. He's my husband's brother, as I already said.'

Jans stepped towards the front door.

'Thank you for giving us the rations, Willem, but I really must get on with the housework now.'

Willem moved with her to the front door and settled an old, grey fedora back on his balding head.

'Oh, I'm sorry, Mevrouw. I didn't mean to hold you up. Please give my greetings to the Dominee and I look forward to meeting his brother in church on Sunday.'

'Yes, goodbye, Willem.'

Jans was surprised, a few minutes later, to come across Peter, sitting at the top of the stairs.

'What are you doing?'

'Just thinking.'

His voice was weary and she climbed up the stairs with some concern.

'What are you thinking about?'

She sat down next to him.

'About the Lord's Supper.'

'Why?'

She was nonplussed. Before he could answer her, Simon and Arend walked in at the front door.

'Hey, what are you two doing, sitting at the top of the stairs?'

Simon was up the steps in a flash and Arend remained at the bottom, grinning at them with his entire six foot three frame.

'Nothing. We're just having a little chat, that's all. And now I'm off to fix lunch.'

Jans got up and walked down the stairs. Peter also stood up.

'Did you have a good walk?'

Simon, cheeks glowing from the outdoors, answered gleefully.

'Yes, and Mrs. Rutger gave us both a peppermint. She also said that Uncle Arend looked a lot like you, Father.'

'Well, I guess that's true enough.'

He paused and then went on to say, 'Arend, could I speak with you a moment in the study?'

'Sure.'

Arend came up, two steps at a time, ruffling Simon's hair as he passed.

'Can I come too?'

Simon was already at the door of the study.

'No, son. I want to speak to Uncle Arend privately.'

Simon pouted.

'Aw, Father.'

'Go and help your mother set the table, Simon.'

And the study door closed.

'Sit down, Arend.'

'Thanks.'

Peter walked over to his desk and sat down behind it. Having the desk in front of him always gave him a feeling of solidity and security. It was, he knew, ridiculous. The desk was wood, after all, and that's all it was. It could be burned, could be destroyed, just like hay and stubble.

'So what did you want to speak to me about? Has Henk been by?'

Arend draped his frame across the chair in front of the desk. Peter was quick to answer.

'No, no, Henk hasn't been by. Why? Did you think that he might have found another place already?'

'Well ...?' Arend's voice was cautious, 'I really don't know.'

There was a bit of a silence.

'It's Thursday today.'

Peter turned his swivel-backed chair around as he spoke and looked out of the window. The main street lay peaceful and an occasional leaf fluttered down onto the road.

'Yes.'

Arend agreed, not knowing where the conversation was leading.

'In three days,' Peter continued, turning back to Arend, 'it will be Sunday. I would ask that you attend worship services with us.'

Arend sat up.

'I see.'

He eyed the man facing him with a certain degree of amusement, a fact which did not escape Peter and one which he found extremely irritating. Arend went on.

'I expect that's what your brother would do, wouldn't he?'

Peter nodded, briefly. 'Yes, that's definitely what a brother of mine would do.'

'Well, since I'm supposed to be your brother, I will gladly do so.'

He stood up, sympathetically adding, 'Were you worried about that, Peter?'

Peter smiled, albeit a trifle thinly, and went on.

'There's more, Arend.'

Arend sat down again.

'What?'

Peter nervously began tapping his fingers on the desk.

'This Sunday we will be celebrating the Lord's Supper.'

'The Lord's Supper?'

'Yes, the Lord's Supper.'

Peter paused and Arend waited.

'We celebrate it several times a year. In it we commemorate the death of our Lord and Saviour, Jesus Christ.'

Arend waved his hand.

'I know what that means, Peter. I may be a Jew and I may be an atheist, but I know what the Lord's Supper means. I ... uh ... I wasn't always an atheist and I'm familiar with Passover and what that means.'

'Oh.'

Peter's interjection was soft, almost lame. Arend went on, slightly incredulous.

'I can't believe that you want me to participate, to take part in your Lord's Supper celebration when I tell you that I don't believe in ...'

Peter stood up, agitated.

'Well, Arend, it seems to me that ...'

'That what?'

Arend stood up too.

'That we ... we might be jeopardizing your position here if you don't. This morning Willem Poske called.'

'Willem who?'

Arend's eyes were fixed on Peter's face. Peter's voice became slightly defensive, a tinge louder, as he answered.

'Willem Poske. We suspect he's a local NSB agent and he asked about you. He asked if you would be going to church; he asked if you would be attending the Lord's Supper; and he asked if he could meet you on Sunday.'

Peter ticked all his worries off on his fingers. Arend walked over to the window and gazed out.

'Look at those leaves, Peter. Look at them flutter and twist in the air. Up and down, up and down. Almost as if they never want to reach the ground. Carried by the wind, gusted here and there. But sooner or later, sooner or later, they land. They all land.'

He then shrugged his shoulders and went on.

'It's all the same to me. The wind carries and sooner or later .., who knows. Sure I'll participate, if that's what you want. I mean, what's the difference. But ...'

He turned and faced Peter directly.

'But surely it must go against your grain to let someone like myself participate.'

Peter did not answer and Arend shrugged again.

'Maybe before Sunday you can fill me in on the exact details. I mean, I wouldn't want to make a mistake.'

His voice dripped with sarcasm. He walked towards the door, but stopped and turned.

'You know, Peter, in the Old Testament, the foreigner, the alien who wanted to participate in the Passover, had to be circumcised. Then, like one born of the land, he was allowed to take part.'

He grinned suddenly.

'I would like you to know that I'm circumcised already.'

Peter stood up. He was suddenly overcome with compassion for Arend's soul and felt ashamed for not having said more.

'Circumcision is also needed for the Lord's Supper,' he responded, 'but the circumcision needed is of the heart not of the flesh. I would dearly like to speak with you about that.'

Arend turned the door handle slowly.

'Maybe some other time,' he answered politely, 'maybe some other time when the war is over.'

There was an elder's meeting that evening. Brother Bakker opened with Scripture reading and prayer. Brother Albert read the minutes of the previous meeting and these were duly approved. Roll call was taken. Brother Henk Ten Wei was marked down as absent, a fact which Peter regretted. The agenda was not lengthy and before too much time had passed the subject of the coming Lord's Supper was broached.

'My brother ...'

Peter began, unsure of whether anyone was actually aware of Arend's true status. 'My brother,' he went on, 'is staying with our family presently. He's from Rotterdam and, even though it is rather short notice, he would like to celebrate the Lord's Supper with us this coming Sunday.'

He stopped rather abruptly and gauged the faces about the table. The air was heavy with cigar smoke.

'Brothers,' he continued, not precisely sure of what he would say, 'I ...'

He stopped again.

'I don't think,' Paul Visser, brother of the doctor, and a kindly man, interrupted him. 'I don't think that the Dominee has to be worried. If you've examined your brother and know him to be a member in good standing, well then, on your word, I think, we can safely permit him to partake.'

Several heads nodded in agreement, although brother Bakker did feel constrained to add, 'This is, of course, an unusual period we are living in.'

This time everyone nodded. It was easy to leave the matter at that. Peter was not required to say any more. Business went on. Correspondence was dealt with. Several miscellaneous items were brought up and the meeting drew to a close. The brothers were anxious to go home.

Later on, in the privacy of their bedroom, under the woollen blankets of their bed, Peter told Jans that Arend would be allowed to participate in the Lord's Supper on Sunday.

'You told all the church elders that he was a Jew?'

Jans was surprised.

'No,' Peter was quick to correct her. 'I just told them that he was my brother ...'

He half-raised himself on his elbow, trying to see her face, wanting her approval, her understanding.

'You're afraid that if Arend doesn't participate, Willem Poske will be breathing down our necks?'

It was not so much a question as a statement.

'Yes. Well no, I'm not worried so much as prudent.'

She didn't say anything for a long while and he could hear her low and measured breathing. He could feel her thinking.

'The Hebrew midwives,' he went on to argue his case, 'lied to protect Hebrew babies and God blessed them.'

Jans plumped up her pillow, also raising herself up on her elbow before she answered rather heatedly.

'That wasn't the same thing at all, Peter Straven.'

'How so?'

Peter was becoming irritated.

'Well,' Jans spoke slowly, 'the Hebrew babies were passive. They weren't required to do anything except live. But Arend ... well, Arend will be active. He'll be eating and drinking ...'

She hesitated before she went on to say, 'He'll be eating and drinking judgment to himself, Peter.'

'Yes, but ...'

Peter's voice had an edge and he continued in a rather shrill whisper.

'What about the fact that we're hiding him? That puts us, as well as Arend, in a certain amount of danger. Remember Rahab and the spies. Rahab lied and she and her household were saved. I've not told the truth. I admit that. I know that. But, you see, if I told all the church elders that we're harbouring a Jew ... Well, I'm just not sure that would have been wise. Don't you see that, Jans?'

She sighed.

'I know you're trying to do what is best, Peter. It's just that ... well, is it entirely necessary to have him partake at all? Surely we could make him out to be ill or something.'

'Willem Poske ...' Peter began.

'Yes, I know,' Jans interrupted. 'But when it comes right down to it, in the long run, the Willem Poskes of this world are no stronger than Goliath was.'

Peter did not sleep well that night. Bleary-eyed and short-tempered, he sat down in his study Friday morning trying to finish off his sermon. Through the window he saw Simon and Arend walk down the street together, off on another walk. The commentary on his desk still lay open at Roman 10. He was doing a series. *'If you confess with your mouth the Lord Jesus, and believe in your heart that God has raised Him from the dead, you shall be saved.'* The wind blew and leaves, like his thoughts, were carried here and there, rising and falling with each gust.

'The Christian position,' he wrote, 'is one that confesses that Jesus is Lord. These are not just to be words, but they imply something.'

He studied the carpet and went on writing.

'And what do they imply? What do they mean?'

He lay down his pen and stood up. The doorbell rang and in spite of himself, he went rigid. A minute later, Jans came up.

'Peter, Henk Ten Wei is here. Can he come up for a minute? He says it won't take long.'

'Of course.'

Peter breathed easier and sat down again behind his desk.

'Sorry to bother you on a Friday morning. I know you're usually putting the finishing touches on your sermon. But I thought you'd like to know that your house guest will be moving on. I already told Jans and she said you'd be happy to hear the news from my own mouth.'

Henk stopped and smiled. Peter smiled too. The smile was a bit strained but relief did embrace him like well-fitting, comfortable shoes.

'When?' he asked.

Henk moved closer to the desk.

'Tonight. I'll be by for him sometime after curfew.'

Peter was surprised.

'That soon?'

'Yes, why? Did you want to keep him a bit longer?'

Henk joked but his eyes, half-serious, studied Peter's face. Peter did not respond.

'Where ... where is he going?'

'Can't really tell you that, Peter. But he'll be in good hands and, I dare say, God willing, he'll make it through the war.'

'God willing,' Peter echoed.

They shook hands and Henk left. Jans came up as soon as he was gone and sat down on the edge of Peter's desk.

'Well,' she said.

'Well, what?'

She smiled.

'Well, are you sorry you asked the church elders about Arend?'

He tapped his pen on the sermon paper.

'Yes and no. I suppose 'yes' because I lied and 'no' because this whole situation is making me realize how weak my faith is, how ...'

He stopped and looked at her sheepishly before he went on.

'Actually, Jans, I am very relieved. And I hate myself for feeling so relieved.'

She hopped off the desk and came to where he sat.

'I was scared too, Peter. And for all his tallness and talk, I'm sure Arend himself has times of fear also. Anyway, I've got to do some housework and Kobus is alone in the playpen downstairs.'

She kissed the top of his head and was gone. Peter looked down at his last notes.

'The Christian position,' he read, 'is one that confesses that Jesus is Lord. These are not just words, but they imply something. And what do they imply? What do they mean?'

After their walk, Simon and Arend came up to the study together.

'Father, can we speak to you?'

'Sure.'

Peter put down his pen, leaning back in his chair. He was almost done with the second point of his sermon and he was beginning to feel better than he had for several days.

'Father?'

Simon walked over to the desk and stood squarely in front of it, his seven-year-old shoulders nudging the wooden side.

'Yes, Simon.'

'Father, Uncle Arend and I were talking. I was telling him about how I played 'end of the war' with Nicholas and Harry and Rolf and I told him about what Harry's mother said about the German soldiers ...'

He paused and turned to look at Arend who was standing in the doorway. Arend nodded at the boy. Simon turned back to his father.

'Then I told Uncle Arend what you said. I mean the part about that the only important thing is to believe in Jesus. And then Uncle Arend said ... He said ...'

The boy's voice faltered and Arend's voice took over.

'I told him that I didn't believe in his Lord Jesus.'

Simon's blue eyes locked hard into Peter's, as Arend continued from where he stood by the door.

'And I also said, that I did not think that a person's love for Jesus was as important to you, Peter, as Simon thought it was.'

A fear gripped Peter's total being for the second time that week. The first fear had come when Henk had asked him to harbour a Jew. It had swept over him, like a river it had swept over him, but he had managed to swim, to survive. But this present fear was far greater. It overwhelmed him; it took his feet away from under him; it choked him; and it threatened to drown him.

'Father!'

Simon looked at him anxiously. Peter had felt somewhat guilty about not speaking directly to the church elders about

Arend. But he had justified it. He had felt even more guilty when he spoke to Jans last night. But he had still managed to justify his action. But now, looking into Simon's clear, blue eyes, he felt positively unclean.

'Father?'

The word had become a question. And what does it matter if a man gains the whole world but loses his soul. And Peter's soul was dying. He knew it was. Expedience was killing it subtly, by degrees, and in the process it would affect those around him.

'Father, why are you not answering me?'

Simon stamped his foot in impatience.

'Because he doesn't know what to say.'

Arend's voice was not sharp, not honed for battle, but it cut nevertheless. Peter stood up.

'Arend is right.'

He spoke heavily and repeated, 'Arend is right. I don't know what to say. I've set a double standard. Son ...'

'Do you mean he is right about the Lord Jesus not being ...'

Simon interrupted, his voice filled with disbelief.

'No, no, son. I didn't mean that.'

Peter walked towards his son and hunched down by him. But Simon backed away.

'What do you mean then?'

'I mean that yesterday I was afraid and I let that fear make me lie.'

Peter's voice shook and he stood up again, hating himself for the surprise he could see in his son's eyes. He swallowed and went on.

'I asked Arend to come to church on Sunday, not so that he could listen to the Gospel but so that nobody would suspect that he was not really my brother.'

He paused and looked at Arend before he went on.

'Not only did I lie but I also asked him to lie, Simon. Arend had told me that he didn't believe in God but I said that because of the danger it didn't matter, that he could pretend to believe in God. That as long as other people thought he believed ... '

His voice trailed off. Out of the corner of his eye he saw the neatly half-written sermon on the desk. It glared at him. It mocked him. 'The Christian position,' he had written, 'is one that confesses that Jesus is Lord.' He turned his body and his heart towards Arend and held out his hand.

'I'm sorry, Arend,' he said, 'I apologize. Will you forgive me? The things I've done and the things I've said are inexcusable.'

Arend took a few steps towards him, smiled and took the proffered hand.

'Forgiven. Like I said yesterday, maybe sometime after the war we can talk. Who knows ... Although you know the old saying, you can't teach an old dog new tricks.'

Peter responded softly, 'Maybe you won't be there after the war, Arend, and old dogs ... well, old dogs, if they're hungry enough, will go for crumbs.'

Arend shrugged and left the room.

'Simon, son, will you forgive me too?'

Simon regarded his father with solemnity.

'Sure, Father. I've lied before. Remember when I broke your pipe and said that I didn't? And when I spilled ink on the tablecloth and I blamed Rolf?'

Peter nodded.

'I remember.'

He hunched down again in front of his son.

'Simon, the worst thing is that I made you think that the Lord Jesus was not important. That was really horrible on my part. The Lord Jesus is more important than anything else.'

Simon did not back away from his father this time.

'I know that Jesus is important. When Uncle Arend said that you didn't believe that, I knew that he must be wrong.'

Jans walked in and Peter stood up.

'Lunch is ready and there's a surprise for my hungry men.'

She smiled at them.

'I'm sorry, Jans.'

Peter's voice was thick with emotion. Jans looked puzzled.

'Why? It's a good lunch. The extra food rations ...'

She stopped and came closer.

'Whatever is the matter with you two? Why are you standing there like that?'

Peter put an arm about her.

'You were right last night, Jans. I'm so sorry. Will you forgive me for giving in to my fears, for not trusting?'

She nodded and leaned her head against his shoulder. It was Peter's third apology.

An hour after Henk picked up Arend that evening, Paul Venter, the local policeman, called at the back door of the parsonage. Jans and Peter were both in the kitchen. Simon and Kobus were in bed.

'Sorry, Dominee, but I've got a warrant for your arrest.'

Jans gripped the back of the chair by which she was standing.

'You've got to be joking, Paul.'

'No, it's no joke.'

He stood rather ill at ease, discomfited by the distress on her face.

'Why?'

She let go of the chair and walked up to Paul.

'Why can't you just let Dominee go? He's got an address. He can go underground.'

Paul shifted from one foot to the other.

'There have already been several arrests tonight, Jans. There are four Nazi soldiers guarding the parsonage outside. The story is that two of our boys stole a car belonging to an SS officer. There was some fighting and I understand that the officer is out for revenge.'

'But why arrest Peter? Why the Dominee?'

Even as Jans spoke, she knew it was a futile question.

'Why anyone?'

Paul answered logically, looking at the ground, avoiding her eyes. Peter walked over to his wife and kissed her.

'I'll probably be back in the morning.'

He tried to make his voice sound trivial, unconcerned.

'Take your heavy coat.'

Jans' anxiety flowed over into activity. She ran into the hall and came back with Peter's winter coat over her arm.

'Here. Put that on. It'll likely be cold in ...'

She stopped and asked Paul.

'Where are you taking him?'

'To the police station. I'll let you know if there's any change.'

He took Peter's arm.

'Time to go, Dominee. I've already been here too long.'

Peter was surprised to see Henk and Arend, as well as Ben and Jan Wassink, two young members of his congregation, sitting cross-legged on the floor of the cell to which he was assigned.

'Hello, Dominee.'

They shook hands and Peter took his place on the floor next to them. A light bulb dangling from the ceiling in the hall cast a dim glow on their faces.

'What exactly happened?' Peter asked.

Henk answered him, briefly.

'Some of our boys needed a car for a raid they were planning. Unfortunately, they were caught. There was some shooting and an SS officer was wounded. Higher up wants revenge and has ordered that at least ten people be rounded up for ...'

'For what?'

'For execution by firing squad.'

Arend completed Henk's unfinished sentence.

'Oh.'

It was all Peter could bring himself to say. They were all quiet for a while.

Then Peter asked, 'Do you know when?'

Henk shook his head.

'No, not really. My guess is tomorrow morning. Probably they'll drive us out to the country, to some field. Who knows?'

Ben Wassink, the youngest person in the group, began to cry. He was sixteen. His brother, who was only eighteen, put an arm around him. Henk looked at Peter. Peter felt a tremendous calm come over him and suggested that they sing. In a soft baritone he began.

As the hart, about to falter,

in its trembling agony.

Henk joined him on the third line.

Longs for flowing streams of water,

so, O God, I long for Thee.

Ben and Jan joined in on fifth line and the singing grew stronger.

Yes, athirst for Thee I cry;

God of life, O when shall I -

come again to stand before Thee,

In Thy temple and adore Thee.

They waited a moment and then went on to the second stanza. There was a peace in the singing – a release of emotions that bowed down before God. By the third stanza Peter experienced a joy such as he had never felt before, a happiness that filled his entire being.

O my soul, why are you grieving,

why disquieted in me?

Hope in God, your faith retrieving:

He will still your refuge be.

Down the hall, in other cells, other male voices began to join them. The rich sound of the forty-second Psalm now filled the corridor.

I again shall laud His grace -
for the comfort of His face:
He will show His help and favour,
for He is my God and Saviour.

One man was not singing. That man was Arend - Arend Straven. He sat next to Peter, head tilted back against the cement wall, eyes closed. He seemed to be listening to the music flowing about him. Peter nudged him after the song.

'Arend?'

Arend shook his head.

'Not now, Dominee Peter, not now. I'm an old dog, remember?'

They sang through most of that night, sang and prayed. There is an eternity of time in the brevity of one single small night when it is known that that night comprises the last night on earth. When souls are confronted with the threshold of eternal life, they can either retreat into themselves and their fears, or they can suddenly be overwhelmed with a desire to honour and praise God abundantly, struck by the fact that He has always been immensely good to them.

When the first white light of dawn lapped in at the high window above Peter's head, ridiculing the dim light bulb in the hall, he saw resignation on the faces of all the men he was with – on all the faces, save Arend's.

'I wonder if ...' Ben's voice trailed off.

'If what?'

His brother's arm lay solidly around his back.

'If we'll be able to see mother and father when we're in heaven ...?'

He looked at Peter. Peter smiled at him.

'I don't know, Ben. Maybe God will give us such a glimpse, but I rather suspect it would make us unhappy. But we can be sure that He will give our loved ones peace.'

'I've always wanted to go to heaven like Elijah.'

Jan spoke up, grinning at his own foolishness, going on to say, 'I like horses and to ride on and up, straight to heaven, to God ...'

'Stop it! Stop it, all of you!'

Arend's voice was grim.

'You're deluded and I'm happy if that makes you happy but must you talk and sing about it all the time? Can't we just be quiet for a little while?'

No one spoke for a minute. Peter was about to say something when there was a commotion in the hall. They heard a child's voice - crying. Peter stood up. He knew that voice.

Suddenly Simon stood in front of the bars of the cell door.

'Father!'

'Simon?'

Peter was on his feet in an instant. Paul Venter stood next to the child.

'They've allowed him in to say goodbye, Dominee. One of the officers here has a son the same age.'

Simon reached his hands through the bars.

'Can't I go in to see my father, Mr. Venter?'

Paul shrugged.

'Don't have the keys, Simon. I can't let you go in even if I wanted to. Now be quick and say your goodbyes because they won't let you stay long.'

Peter enfolded his son's hands and felt a small wad of paper between their palms. The boy stared at him, tear stains on his cheeks.

'Thank you for coming, Simon. How is Mother?'

'She told me to tell you that she loves you very much.'

Simon's voice trembled and he went on, 'And so do I love you, Father.'

Peter nodded, his heart too full to be able to speak properly.

'And baby Kobus?' he finally managed.

'The baby is fine. Oh, Father ...! Oh, Father!'

The boy's hands were clammy with sweat and Peter clasped them hard.

'You are the man of the house now, Simon. Take care of Mother and the baby. Remember you can't do it alone. Always, always, pray to the Lord, son, and He will help you.'

'Yes, Father.'

Simon was sobbing now and Paul Venter ran the back of his hand across his nose.

'It's time for him to go, Dominee.'

Simon pressed Peter's hands hard and the wad of paper imprinted on Peter's right palm. He closed that hand and pushed Simon's hands back through the bars.

'If not on earth, son, I will see you in heaven - in the new Jerusalem.'

Paul Venter led the boy away who looked over his shoulder at his father until the corridor swallowed him up.

Peter hesitated a moment before he sat down again. He put his right hand into his pocket and dropped the paper into it. Maybe it was a note from Jans - maybe from Simon. Better wait a moment until he knew for sure that no guards were coming back this way. He sat down again on the floor between Henk and Arend. Arend had his eyes closed. The corridor remained quiet. Carefully Peter put his hand into his pocket and unfolded the small paper, smoothing it with his fingers. It was small, easily fitting within the parameters of the lining. He inched it out slowly, moving it onto his knees. Looking down without moving his head, he felt a tremendous surge of disappointment when he saw that the paper was blank - totally blank. He sighed.

'Turn it around, Dominee.'

Henk, at his left, whispered advice. Peter turned the paper. There was writing, Jans' writing, very small writing. He strained to read.

'When you feel the second curve in the road,' her voice whispered off the paper, 'jump out of the truck. The back door will be unlocked. Run to the right. Fall into the ditch. Help forthcoming.'

Peter read the paper twice and then showed it to Henk. Henk studied it for a minute, then crumpled it up and put it into his shoe. He grinned at Peter and, whispering quietly, they divulged the message to the others in the cell.

Fifteen minutes later a German guard called for Arend Straven. Arend stood up. He glanced at the others, and said, 'Well, it's been nice.'

'God go with you, Arend.'

Henk stood up as well and offered Arend his hand. The others also shuffled to their feet and awkwardly took turns saying goodbye. The guard became impatient.

'Schnell, Jude.'

Arend blanched and stepped towards the door, following the guard out into the corridor. The door shut and no one said anything until the footsteps had died away. Peter looked at Henk.

'How did they ...?'

Henk sighed in answer.

'I honestly don't know. I have no idea.'

Ben nervously ran his hand through his hair.

'Do you think that the plan for jumping out of ... '

'Shh.'

The warning came simultaneously from Henk and Jan.

'Don't talk about it.'

They sat quietly for the next half hour, each thinking his own thoughts, each busy with different matters, until footsteps brought them all to their feet once again. Arend was led back in. His eyes were swollen, his jaw was bruised, his shirt had been ripped and burn marks were evident on his right arm. The guard grinned.

'Get ready to travel - all of you. All of you that is except that one there,' and he pointed to Arend before he continued with, 'That one we'll probably shoot in the public square here in Hartenhand as an example of Aryan cleansing.'

Arend leaned against the wall. The guard had closed the door and left. No one spoke and Peter found himself taking off his winter coat. The buttons felt big and clumsy to his fingers. They were difficult to undo. He could see Jans running out to the hall to make sure that he wore it. Weather-wise it hadn't been necessary. It wasn't very cold outside yet. But he had kept it on all night until now. The last button came undone. Walking over to Arend, who still stood hunched against the wall, he draped the coat over the torn shirt. Arend looked at him. His right eye was beginning to turn black.

'Trying to cover my Jewishness?'

Peter did not respond but pulled Arend away from the wall, motioning to Henk that he needed help. Henk came over, a puzzled expression on his face.

'What are you doing, Peter? What do you have in mind?'

Peter answered quietly, but they could all hear him.

'I'm changing places with him. We're pretty much the same build and size. With my coat on and with his head down, and with you walking in front and behind him, surely he can make it to the truck. He'll have a chance that way.'

Arend, his right hand in the sleeve of Peter's coat, suddenly began to cry.

'A crumb, is it? Feeding me a crumb. Well, I'll eat it. I'll eat it and, who knows, it might just save me. Who knows.'

Henk lifted his eyebrows and helped Arend put his left hand into the coat. There was no time to talk further. They could all hear commotion out in the corridor again. Instinctively Peter lay down in the far right corner of the cell, face to the wall.

'Achtung, achtung. Prisoners will line up and march, single file, down the hall.'

Peter closed his eyes and prayed, 'Dear Father in heaven, help us all in this time of need.'

His hands were sweaty and he could feel beads of perspiration drip down his forehead. If there was a righteousness by works, then surely, surely, he would be saved. But there was no such thing as righteousness by works and this one act, this one act alone, could and would not save him. Only Jesus could do that. The cell door opened.

'Achtung, march straight ...'

Would they notice Arend? Peter's form was rigid. If they did, they'd all be in serious trouble. As if they weren't already. 'Dear Father in heaven, help us all in this time of need.' He could hear Henk begin singing.

But the Lord will send salvation,

and by day His love provide.

The footsteps and the voices began to die away.

He shall be my exultation,

and my song at eventide.

And then there was quiet.

When his identity was discovered by a guard, almost an hour later, Peter was kicked and beaten in the cell. He was then taken away to an interrogation room. An older SS officer who was to examine him, regarded him quizzically and then invited him to sit down.

'You are ... Peter Straven, *pfarrer*, ja ... minister to the people of this village?'

'Yes, yes, I am.'

'Cigaret?'

'No, thank you.'

The burn marks on Arend's arm came to mind and the bruises on his own shins and shoulders lay hot and sore. Involuntarily, Peter shuddered.

'*Du bist kalt?* Cold? Maybe you should have taken a coat to the prison? Ja?'

Peter shook his head. Was the man playing with him?

'No, I'm not cold, thank you.'

He didn't know why he kept saying thank you.

'So you were friends with this Jewish man and now you think he will escape? Do you not realize that he, as well as the others, will be shot as soon as the truck reaches its destination. Perhaps he is dead already.'

He regarded Peter through narrowed eyelids while he twirled a letter opener in his hands.

'I will ask you again. You knew this Jew? You were friends with this man?'

Peter considered the questions, tossed them over in his mind. Did it matter to deny? Would a lie save him? Probably not. Besides, had he not learned that the truth was more important than his own line of reasoning, that it was more important than fear? He took a deep breath.

'Yes, I knew him.'

The officer leaned forward on his elbow. The letter opener poised in his hand like a small sword.

'So you knew him. But surely you knew that to harbour a Jew, a dog, is an offense, an offense punishable by death?'

The officer smiled a slow smile at him, put down the letter opener and adjusted the small glasses on his nose.

Peter managed to smile back and asked, 'Do you believe in God and His only Son, Jesus Christ?'

The officer was taken aback.

'Do I believe in God ... in Jesus? Of course I do. When I was a child I even attended the Lutheran church. Always my mother prayed ...'

Peter interrupted.

'If you believe in God, sir, then by your own standards, you are guilty of death. For if you confess Jesus, sir, you harbour a Jew in your heart.'

The officer took off his glasses and stood up. He walked around the desk and stared long and hard at Peter.

'You have much courage ... but ....'

He did not finish the sentence. A weariness flooded Peter. What did it all matter? What did it all avail in the long run? But a voice came to him from within his inner being. 'Do not fear those who can kill the body, rather fear Him who ...'

'You are preaching tomorrow?'

The officer was sitting on the edge of the desk now, right in front of Peter.

'Yes ... that is to say ...'

Peter stopped. The officer got off the desk.

'Perhaps I will come to your church. Stand up, please.'

Peter stood up and the officer continued, 'Just to make sure that there are no misunderstandings for those who oppose the Reich ...'

The next instant Peter felt the man's fist crack against his jaw, once, twice, three times. He steadied himself against the chair, saw black and lost consciousness. When he came to, the officer was sitting behind the desk again, peering through his bifocals, calmly reading a newspaper. Peter lay for a while, regarding the man from his prone position. His head throbbed and when he cautiously tried to raise it, pain exploded behind his eyes.

'I'm confident,' the officer spoke quietly and without looking at him, 'that you will preach well tomorrow.'

Peter half-sat up. The room swam. He crawled back to his chair on his knees. The officer put down his newspaper.

'You are free to go, Herr *pfarrer*.'

'Free ...? But why?'

Peter's voice was hoarse and he tasted blood in his mouth. Was there some trick? Was this a devilish plot to raise hopes and then dash them again? The officer stood up. He put his glasses down onto the desk.

'There are many wars ...'

He paused and then went on, 'The most difficult are those wars ... which are waged within the heart of man ...'

Peter unsteadily got to his feet. Perhaps the man was mad. The officer picked up his glasses and began playing with them.

'Go,' he said, 'go and preach, Herr *pfarrer*. Go and feed the sheep.'

He turned abruptly.

And Peter went.

'You have multiplied, O Lord my God, your wondrous deeds and your thoughts toward us; none can compare with you! I will proclaim and tell of them, yet they are more than can be told.'
Psalm 40:5

AND AFTERWARDS I KNEW

Providence is a strange and wonderful thing. It is able to take on proportions as small as a raindrop or as large as an air raid; it is able to appear as seemingly insignificant as a rip in a tablecloth or as conspicuous as a thunderstorm: but whether small or large, insignificant or conspicuous, providence is always within the confines of God's intricate plan for the good of His people and to the glory of His name.

* * *

Anne Groen was hanging up laundry on the clothesline in her backyard. Although a windy day in April, the spring sun seemed to foreshadow a lovely summer. Her five-year-old son rode his tricycle along the flag-stoned path leading to the driveway and three-year-old Emma played in the sandbox. Spring was in the air. Robins sang and the sky was blue. Anne sighed deeply as she leaned over the wooden railing of the deck. Contentment filled her. The clothes flapped in the breeze.

'Hey, Mom - Mommy.'

Brian called loudly as he peddled past.

'Yes, honey. I see you.'

Not to be outdone by her brother, Emma waved enthusiastically from the sandbox. Anne waved back. She stood on the deck a moment longer, watching her children, before she turned to open the kitchen door.

'I'm going inside now, guys,' she called, 'Stay in the backyard.'

Around ten o'clock Anne took her children shopping. The wind had picked up and thunder clouds no bigger than a man's fist knocked on the horizon. But with the wind blowing so steadily surely any rain would pass. She dawdled in the aisles of the supermarket and relaxed in the chatter of her offspring as she stood in line at the grocery checkout.

'Look, Mom, it's raining.'

Fat drops hit the supermarket's large windows, and Anne's thoughts travelled to her backyard, to the sheets and pillowcases which were, no doubt, undergoing a second rinse.

'Oh, well, the sun'll be out again soon.'

Optimistically she smiled at the cashier, paid for her groceries and drove back home while the children sang, 'Rain, rain, go away, Come again some other day.'

'What day, Mom?'

'Oh, I don't know. How about tomorrow?'

'Tomorrow's Sunday. Then we'll be in church.'

'Yes, we will.'

'When it rains on Sunday, is that work for God, Mom?'

'No, Brian. I don't think so.'

Brian did not press the question with his usual 'Why not?' refrain and she was thankful for it. He could be theologically challenging, especially within the confines of the car when she needed all her attention for the road.

'The clothes will be wet again, Mom.'

'Yes, but they will dry again soon later this afternoon. Hey, that rhymes.'

Brian and Emma laughed as the car turned into the driveway. The rain had stopped and the sun was making a rather pale appearance.

'Can we play outside, Mom. Please!'

'All right.'

Anne carried the groceries in through the front door as Brian and Emma ran to the backyard. She had barely made it to the kitchen, arms full of bags, when Brian frantically pounded on the back door.

'Mommy, come quick.'

Anne opened the back door and immediately saw that her entire wash line had snapped and fallen to the ground. It lay in a fairly straight line, sodden and flat. Although an optimist at heart, she could not help but sigh deeply as she leaned against the door.

'Oh, well, I guess I'll have to do the laundry again. But first Mom'll take in the groceries. Keep an eye on Emma, will you, Brian?'

Some fifteen minutes later Anne walked outside with the clothes hamper to pick up the fallen laundry. In the distance she heard the neighbour's door open and close and within seconds a big, black dog bounded into the yard.

'A dog, Mom, a dog!'

Brian and Emma were both delighted and apprehensive, as the lab alternately sniffed and licked them. They patted him carefully.

'Good dog.'

A woman appeared at the hedge separating the properties.

'Ach, the hund is by your yard! Sorry!! Peter!! Peter, komm!!'

But the young lab had no intention of coming and, wagging his tail, he playfully ran circles around the children. Suddenly the line of fallen laundry caught his eye and scooping up the edge of a tablecloth, he began to pull it across the lawn, shaking it fiercely, daring the children to take the other end.

'Nein, no Peter!'

The woman's voice was shocked and she ran along the privet hedge dividing the two properties until she came to a small opening. Peter had, by now, dragged the tablecloth towards the driveway, Brian and Emma shrieking behind him.

'Mom! Mom! Look at the dog!'

Anne was at a loss as to what to do. The woman was in her yard now, continually and frantically calling the dog.

'Komm, Peter! Komm here.'

Suddenly the dog let go of the tablecloth and cantered towards his mistress. She grabbed his collar and held fast. Looking at Anne, she said,

'I'm very sorry. Please forgive me. I bring Peter back now.'

She turned and walked back towards her house. Anne watched her go. Brian tried to lift the bedraggled tablecloth.

'It's pretty dirty, Mom.'

The tablecloth was special. It didn't actually belong to Anne but was a communal tablecloth, used for the Lord's Supper table at church. The women of the congregation took turns washing and ironing it prior to Communion. Anne washed it again that afternoon but two large rips and several grass stains made her a little queasy about what the final result would be. The children had gone to the library with Donald, her husband, but the quiet in the house was not conducive towards giving her a solution. The front doorbell rang. Upon opening the door she came face to face with the dog's owner for the second time that day. The woman was holding a large parcel wrapped in brown paper.

'For you.'

Without further ado, she handed the parcel over to Anne.

'For me?'

Anne held onto the brown wrapping with a mixture of uncertainty and curiosity.

'Yes.'

'Won't you come in please?'

'Nein, no.'

'Please.'

Anne smiled as she spoke and then continued.

'We don't really know one another and I would be so happy to have you drink a cup of tea with me.'

The woman hesitated and Anne opened the door wider.

'I've just put the kettle on. I'd love to have you come in.'

Impulsively she put out her hand.

'I'm Anne Groen.'

The woman put out her hand also, returning the smile. She was perhaps somewhere in her fifties. Wavy black hair tied back into a bun, a high, smooth forehead, brown eyes, a straight nose, high cheekbones and beautifully formed lips, all combined to form a gentle face.

'Dora Hubner.'

'Well, please come in, Mrs. Hubner.'

The parcel contained a beautiful, ivory-coloured tablecloth. Its four corners all had exquisitely embroidered crosses embroidered on them. The material's silky essence rippled like water in Anne's hands and she sensed that the linen was very valuable.

'I couldn't possibly take it.'

Dora Hubner smiled.

'My dog has done great harm. I have seen it. And I am happy to give this to you. Please, you make me very happy.'

'Did you make it yourself?'

'Jawohl[10]. Many years ago when I was a bride. You see in the corner have I put my initials, DEH. Very small. This means Dora Erika Hubner.'

Anne carefully folded the tablecloth and lay it aside on the edge of the couch. She poured the tea and sat down beside her guest.

'How long have you been in Canada?'

'I came in 1953.'

Anne smiled.

'I emigrated from Holland with my parents in 1948. I was fifteen.'

Mrs. Hubner said nothing. Her hands wrapped the teacup. Anne tried again.

'We, that is my family and I, were all very excited to be moving to Canada. My dad's first job was in Chatham. He picked tomatoes for a few months. He's hated tomatoes ever since.'

She laughed and Mrs. Hubner smiled. Encouraged Anne probed again.

'What did your husband do? Did he have a sponsor?'

'Mine husband?'

Anne smiled and nodded.

'Yes, what was his first job when he came to Canada?'

'I came alone. He is not here. He ... died before I came.'

Her hands gripped the teacup again and she looked away from Anne at the carpet.

---

[10] Jawohl - German word for yes.

'I'm sorry. You must miss him.'

To Anne's dismay she saw a tear roll down Mrs. Hubner's cheek.

'I'm sorry,' she repeated lamely.

Mrs. Hubner put down her tea and wiped her cheek.

'Nein, do not be sorry. It is your fault not. The tablecloth ....'

She stopped. Anne picked up the tablecloth from where it lay folded over on the arm of the couch.

'It's so beautiful. I really think you should take it back. I couldn't accept such a gift. It obviously means a lot to you.'

'I will the story tell you of the tablecloth. Ja, I will tell you the story. Please sit and listen.'

Anne sat back, her eyes fixed on her guest. Mrs. Hubner leaned back also.

'I am German-Canadian. You know this. You can by my speech tell. I was in Hamburg born - many years ago - in 1910. I became nurse. My parents died when I was in training and I was alone. But then I met Stefan - Stefan Hubner. He was a doctor and we were married on the 13th of February, 1932. We moved to Dresden.'

Mrs. Hubner stopped. She reached for and took a sip from her tea.

'Dresden?' Anne repeated the name of the city.

'Yes, Dresden. You know this place? It is very beautiful. Grosser Garten was wonderful in the spring. The River Elbe had terraces where you could watch the ships go by. We had the Schloss, a big castle and the Frauenkirche ... that is ... that was where we to church went. Many trees lined the streets ... the Pragerstrasse was ...'

She stopped again. Anne smiled.

'It sounds like a place you loved.'

'Ja. I did. I had my home there ... Mein children ... my children ...'

'Where are your children now?'

Anne bit her tongue. Stupid question. Any half-wit would have deduced that the children were dead ... the war ... Mrs. Hubner did not answer but looked down again.

'I tell you more.'

'You don't have to tell me, Mrs. Hubner. I can see that it is very difficult for you ...'

'Nein, perhaps it is gut to speak. Perhaps it will ...'

She paused again and then went on.

'We had zwei, two, children - zwei tochter, girls, Ursula und Erika. It was a good leben[11]. They were healthy. We were not really affected very much by the noises of war until 1939. Stefan was busy in the hospital. I was busy at home. But in 1939 Stefan was called up to serve in the Polish campaign. He did not want to go but ...'

'That must have been hard.'

Anne spoke softly. She had read about Poland. She felt strange. Here was a woman whose husband had worn a Nazi uniform, albeit unhappily. Mrs. Hubner looked at her.

'You do not understand. Anyway, Stefan stayed not in the army very long. He had a lung disease and was to a sanatorium sent. It was not until 1944 that he cured was and back came to Dresden. We were so very happy to see him. He could again work in the hospital in Dresden.'

Anne couldn't help but interrupt.

'You never in all those years wondered about Hitler ... about other things ... about Jews?'

---

[11] Leben - German word for life.

'Some people in Dresden said Hitler began the war and
that he Jews killed. In other countries know they this better
but you will not believe me. But these things were secret kept.
You could even punished be if you used not 'Heil Hitler' in
greeting. Once told I a joke in a cloakroom - a political joke
- and the Gestapo has me ten hours questioned. They asked
me and asked me things. I escaped barely from being sent to
a concentration camp. They have warned me that my name
on the black list was. I thought then that a concentration
camp was latrine cleaning and other work. About what really
happened I know it now - but then, no, I knew it not.'

'Oh.'

It was all Anne replied and then she added, 'Are you ...
was your family Christian?'

'Yes, we go to the church every Sunday. And we pray. We
pray very much. The Frauenkirche services had twice. We
passed the statue of Martin Luther before the kirche and my
girls would say 'Who is this man?' And I tell them.'

'And your husband was cured? His lungs were better?'

'Yes, he worked hard at the hospital after his years at the
sanatorium. He was not a member of the Party.'

There was silence in the room. It had begun to rain again
and the drops touched the window gently. Anne got up to
light the lamps and then sat down again. Mrs. Hubner stared
at the rain and continued speaking.

'I will now tell you about the tablecloth. How I still have
it. It was a long time ago ... but like yesterday. Yes, fifteen
years ...'

She sighed and folded her hands. Anne looked at her
anxiously.

'If you would rather not speak of it, Mrs. Hubner. I can
understand ...'

'Nein, it is gut. I did not plan to speak but the tablecloth that I give you ... I think that it should belong to ....'

Anne interrupted.

'Oh, but it will belong to my church. You see, it was my turn to wash the Communion tablecloth. It covers the table for the Lord's Supper. Do you know ...'

'Lord's Supper? Ja, I know what that means and I think this is maybe something ... something very gut.'

The rain poured and Mrs. Hubner smiled at Anne.

'It was a Tuesday. It was 13th February in 1945. Also our anniversary. We had been ten years married. I was at home. We lived in a house on the corner of Parkstrasse and Tiergartenstrasse. This was close to the zoo. We had a wonderful zoo in Dresden and I took the girls often there. But at this time the girls were with my uncle in Murnau in Bavaria. The Russians were coming closer and closer and we, Stefan and I, thought they would be safer there - farther away from the border. Stefan wanted that I also should leave on the train to be with them. He got me a seat on the train that was to leave Dresden that evening of 13th February at ten o'clock. He took me himself to the train station. I had some clothes in a suitcase and some rice ... there was not much food. Stefan would go back home to bury our valuables before the Russians come. Stefan, he could not himself come. They would say he was a deserter.'

'The train stood waiting at the station. I went on the train and sat down on a seat - a seat by a window. There was outside a clock and everyone kept looking at the clock because the train should leave, even when an air raid warning began. Then the loudspeakers said the train could not leave. We thought that was perhaps because people were climbing through the windows into the train. You see many wanted to leave Dresden. All the lights were now out and the station was very dark. No one was still outside – only my Stefan stood still by my window. He wanted not to go until the train left. But then went he too.'

Anne coughed. She visualised herself on that train and Donald on the station platform. Mrs. Hubner continued.

'I could the planes hear over the city. It was an air raid. Some people on the train wanted to stay and others wanted to leave. I broke my window. It was made of cardboard and I crawled through the window with my suitcase. Others followed me. We ran over the platform but there were barriers set up around the train station. We climbed over. There were police on the road who urged us to go back to the air raid shelter at the station. But we ran across the road. We wanted very much to be away from the station. There was a school – a technical school across the road. It had also a shelter and there were already many people. We crowded together. A few minutes later this school was hit. There was dust and smoke and pieces of ceiling dropped down on us. But we lived ... that is to say, I lived. Many died. More than three thousand dead were the next day at the railway station found and three hundred dead on the train were found. They were all burnt to death.'

Mrs. Hubner shifted her position slightly. Anne listened wide-eyed.

'We all left the shelter later – the ones who lived. When the 'all-clear' sirens went we left. In the street saw I that every second house on fire was. People screamed. There was smoke. I made my way back to our house. It was difficult. You could not see more than five steps ahead. Trees and broken wires lay everywhere. Many people walked to Grosser Garten where we lived. They carried bundles and pushed prams. Finally I came to our house. It still stood but the doors and windows were blown out. Stefan was there too. He was happy to see me. He brought our mattresses and blankets down to the cellar. He brought down other things - the radio, some paintings, a few small carpets and ... and he brought ...'

She stopped and Anne added softly, '... the tablecloth?'

Mrs. Hubner nodded. 'Yes, the tablecloth. He thought it very beautiful and always called it our special tablecloth ... for happy times ... birthdays, anniversaries ... and it was that very day our anniversary. It was a tablecloth for celebrating ...'

She looked at Anne who nodded, sat back and waited.

'The second attack came a little after midnight. Our house in Parkstrasse was full of people because it was standing yet. The planes flew over us again and again. There was no end to it. And then was there a hit and the house was suddenly on fire. Stefan took us outside and he made the tablecloth wet and wrapped it around me. We walked down Tiergartenstrasse. We had to keep on walking. All around us time bombs exploded. There were many corpses. But I saw not much because Stefan had wrapped the tablecloth around me. We walked on and on and in the early morning reached Nothitz. This is south of Dresden and the Grosser Garten and well-clear of the city. Behind us there was only the burning - only fire. We stayed at a friend's house and then, the next day Stefan went back to Dresden – to the hospital.'

'Why?'

The question slipped out before Anne knew it.

'Because he must. There were too many ill. People were blind from fire and dust. But there were more air attacks that day and Stefan ...'

'Oh, I'm sorry.'

It was all Anne could muster. Outside the rain grew heavier, as if weeping uncontrollably.

'Did you go back to Dresden?'

'After the attack rain came. As now it rains here. They have said to me that it always rains after a bombing. Dresden was a sea of mud and corpses. Yes, I go to look. The hospital was bombed.'

'And after that did you go to your uncle's home where you had sent your daughters?'

'I became ill and friends cared for me in Dresden. I was ill for some time. The centre of Dresden was blocked off and the dead bodies were burnt on grids set on fire by army flamethrowers. For weeks I saw men pass the house I was in. They were pushing carts. The carts held wooden boxes, cardboard boxes, paper parcels, and suitcases. These containers all held human parts that had been found and they were taken to be burned. Later I went to look for my daughters and my uncle. But they were gone. They also were killed. I cannot now speak of it.'

Anne moved closer and laid her right hand on Mrs. Hubner's hands.

'I am sorry. And I am glad you are here now. Thank you for the gift of the tablecloth.'

There were lame words. She felt them to be lame. But Mrs. Hubner's hands took hers.

'The tablecloth I give. And it makes me glad that it will be on God's table. I give it to Him then. It is a giving table, is it not? And so I give Him the pain of the tablecloth. It is much pain. It is my life.'

She let go of Anne's hands.

'Now I must go.'

They stood up simultaneously.

'Thank you for telling me about your life. I didn't know you had moved next door. I hope I'll see you again.'

'I live not there. I bring a visit to a friend for a few days.'

'Well, maybe I'll see you again before you leave? You are welcome for tea again and I would really like you to meet my husband.'

Mrs. Hubner smiled. She walked towards the door and held out her hand.

'Goodbye, Frau Groen. Thank you for the tea.'

'You're welcome.'

The door closed behind Mrs. Hubner and, standing by the window, Anne watched her walk away through the rain. Donald pulled into the driveway shortly afterwards. Emma and Brian raced to the front, giggling in their excitement about getting wet. Donald followed a minute later, cheerfully dripping all over the carpet. It was not really the time to tell him about Dresden, about Mrs. Hubner and about the tablecloth. Later, when the kids had settled down with their library books, she did tell him. But he was not as impressed, not as moved, as she wanted him to be. Unaccountably, this angered her somewhat.

Although Anne had planned to bring the tablecloth to Mrs. Stark, the church custodian, herself, she asked Donald if he would mind driving that evening. It was still pouring rain outside and she was tired.

'Sure, hon.'

'And could you also go by the supermarket and pick up some butter. I forgot to get some this morning and maybe you could get some apple juice as well.'

Donald grinned.

'Sure, hon. Anything else?'

Brian and Emma waved to their father from the window. Lightning streaked across the sky. Out of the corner of his eye Donald saw Anne draw the curtains as he drove away. The windshield wipers could barely keep up with the rain.

'Well, I guess I'll head for the store first. It's just past the Starks' house and I'll stop there on my way back.'

Donald frequently spoke to himself, sang out loud and waved at strangers with the philosophy of 'Who knows whether or not they might be angels.'

The store was almost empty. Donald found the butter and apple juice, paid at the checkout and carefully made his way past puddles back to the car. Slowly inching out of the parking lot, he noted the lone figure of a man, straddling an impossibly huge umbrella, at the bus stop. Impulsively he stopped and rolled down the window.

'Can I give you a lift?'

The man hesitated and then nodded. Donald instinctively knew that, were it not for the incredibly heavy downpour, he would not have accepted. Leaning over, he opened the passenger door. The man shut his umbrella and quickly got in. He was middle-aged, possibly somewhere in his fifties.

'I'm Donald.'

Donald extended his right hand and the man, after standing his umbrella next to him against the seat, point up, shook it firmly.

'Steven.'

'Nice to meet you, Steven. It's pretty wet out.'

'Yes, it is.'

'Well, where can I take you?'

'I live on John Street.'

'Well, hey, that's just two blocks from where I live. Glad to give you a ride. But I have to stop by someone's house first and drop off a parcel. I hope you don't mind the bit of extra time?'

'No, that's fine. I appreciate the lift.'

It was only a block back to the Starks' house and Donald pulled into their driveway slowly. The rainfall had increased in intensity and the wipers gave him very little visibility. 'I think we'll just sit for a minute. It's bound to let up.'

Steven was agreeable.

'Sure.'

Donald reached into the back for the package with the tablecloth. Anne had wrapped it in a brown paper bag. It was rather unwieldy and, on second thought, Donald thought it better to let it stay where it was for the time being.

'We take turns doing the church laundry.'

His passenger did not respond, but Donald, naturally talkative, did not give up.

'Do you go to a church?'

'No. God has forgotten me and I have forgotten God.'

The statement came out with no feeling, as if it was a weather report, such as 'cloudy today – no sunshine expected tomorrow.' Steven stared straight ahead. Donald was at a loss for words, and carefully thought out what he should say next. Before Donald could formulate a reply the garage light in front of them was turned on and the garage door opened. Mrs. Stark beckoned the car in. Donald was relieved.

'Well, that's good. I won't have to get the package wet, after all.'

It was a small garage. Mrs. Stark stood on the passenger side.

'Would you mind rolling down your window and giving her the laundry?'

Steven obliged and rolled down his window. Donald passed the package to the front. It was an awkward exercise and in the process the parcel fell from his hand, hitting the sharp point of the umbrella. The wrapping tore. A small piece of tablecloth crept out. Donald's hands reached down.

'Oh dear! Well, no harm done. Let's just tuck ...'

Steven's hands, however, were quicker than his and he had picked up the bulky package from the floor. He held it a moment as if he were cradling a child. Then, taking the exposed slip of tablecloth between the thumb and index finger of his right hand, he stared. Initials spilled onto his ring finger, the cross rippled into his palm and he wept.

'Jesus said to her,
"I am the resurrection and the life.
Whoever believes in me, though he die, yet shall he live,
and everyone who lives and believes in me
shall never die.
Do you believe this?"'
John 11:25-26

FOUR DAYS IN THE LIFE OF ALBERT TENFOLD

Albert ran his hand over the thin paper page of his Bible and cleared his throat. *'Now for the matters you wrote about: It is good for a man not to marry. But since there is so much immorality, each man should have ...'* He always felt slightly uncomfortable reading this passage.

'What's the matter?' his mother asked. 'Do you have a sore throat?'

'No, Mother. I don't'

Regal and straight, his mother sat across from him in the red, high-backed plush chair which had been his stepfather's. She peered at him through her bifocals.

'Shouldn't let your thoughts wander, Albert.'

He cleared his throat again and continued to read.

'... should have his own wife, and each woman her own husband.'

His mother's voice picked up where he had left off. They took turns reading two verses each after meals. He regarded her for a moment as she read, ringed hands on her lap. It was one of the few moments he could observe her without her knowledge. Her rather coarse face had an equally coarse voice. Loud, but monotonous, it had very little inflection. She hadn't gone to school here, so perhaps the English ... But then, when she read in Dutch, she had the same tone.

Her grey, rheumy eyes suddenly met his.

'Albert, where are your thoughts tonight? Verse five, child.'

He found the place and went on.

'Do not deprive each other except by mutual consent ...'

As he read, his thoughts smoothed out the ridges which he occasionally tripped over. And when he later read *'for it is better to marry than to burn with passion ...'* he was able to keep his mind on Paul without focusing on the lack of passion in his own life – a passion he occasionally desired.

Before Albert cleared the table, he helped his mother to the couch.

'Do you want the paper? Or shall I turn on the television for you?'

She shook her head to both questions.

'I'm a bit tired, son. I think I'll have a small nap while you do the dishes. In that way I'll be fresh for Scrabble when Mrs. Dorman comes later. Be sure to set out the cups for tea and the cookies ...'

'I know, Mother. I know.'

There was a certain resignation in his voice as he pulled the afghan over her body but a thin thread of irritation wound its way to his hands and a sudden clumsiness overtook them.

In the kitchen Paul's words swam about as he placed the dishes in the sink.

' ... it is better to marry than to burn with passion ...'

Had Paul known more about passion than he did? Had Paul been married? Had he taken a wife with him on his missionary journeys? – or a mother? And if Paul had taken his mother ... He suddenly grinned at the suds but then became serious. What did he, Albert, know about marriage anyway? His expertise lay in being single. He scrubbed at the potato pan with increased vigour and some frustration. The small kitchen surrounded him with apathy. There was nothing new. Coffee mugs hung on a small rack in the same way that they had hung for years and years. A birthday calendar, with numerous Dutch aunts and uncles, hung beside it. The refrigerator shone bravely and the square tiles on the floor reflected cleanliness and care. The wooden plaque on the wall spoke to him in Peter's voice, *'Cast all your care upon Him for He careth for you.'*

'But what are my cares, Peter?'

Albert questioned the plaque out loud and repeated his words a trifle noisier than he actually meant.

'What are my cares?'

'What's that, Albert? I can't hear you.'

'Nothing, Mother. Just go to sleep.'

'I'm sure you said something.'

'No, Mother.'

He folded the dish towel over the rack and walked back into the living room.

'Are you sure you didn't say something, Albert?'

'Yes, Mother. I'm sure.'

He stood in the middle of the room, undecided as to what to do.

'Sit down, son, and read the paper.'

'I'm going out tonight, Mother.'

'Out? But Mrs. Dorman ...'

'She's your friend, Mother. She's coming to play Scrabble with you ...'

'But you always play with us. She ...'

'I'm going out tonight, Mother.'

His voice was firm.

'But where are you going?'

She half sat up, reaching for the bifocals on the side table.

'I'm going out.'

It was all Albert could manage.

'But ...'

'You'll be all right. And I'll be home in good time.'

He was out in the hall before she could formulate a reply.

'Albert?'

Opening the closet door, he took his coat off a hanger.

'Albert?'

Her voice was becoming louder.

'I'll see you later, Mother.'

The door handle felt cold under his hand and the hinges squeaked.

'Albert?'

It was more of a shout this time and he shut the door firmly, feeling both guilt and relief.

* * *

Albert Tenfold lived on the fifth floor of a high-rise apartment building with his widowed mother. He was thirty-five and she was seventy. His stepfather had died when he was a teenager. Cast into the mold of male provider at an early age, he had never really been young. Fiercely dependent, his mother had leaned on him heavily, and he had settled under the weight. To the outward eye, they were a model family – a stalwart son providing constant love and care for an aging, frail mother. And it had seemed that way to Albert also, had seemed that way until this last month. Perhaps because he was rapidly approaching his thirty-sixth birthday, he had been doing some thinking. Ten years from now he would be forty-five, and his mother would be eighty and then, ten years later, he would be in his mid-fifties and she would be ninety. Unless she died, but somehow he could not envisage his mother dead, even though deep down he sometimes wished it. He would be her son forever – her son and not someone's husband, someone's father. And then guilt would flood over him like a wave of hot wind and he would break out in a sweat. How could he be thinking such thoughts?

The hall was empty. As he plodded towards the elevator, Albert did up the buttons of his coat. It had all been very well to tell Mother that he was going out, but the truth was that he had no inkling of where he would go. He had few friends – few friends outside his mother's circle, that is. There were a great many Mrs. Dormans: widows who delighted in visiting back and forth; who excelled in speaking of rheumatism, arthritis and the weather; and who always commented on how fortunate his mother was to have him. The elevator had brought him down to the first floor. He walked towards the front door. It was raining and he stood for a moment, contemplating the sidewalk through the heavy glass doors. He could go to the library. As he opened the door, the sound of the rain comforted him. It was a sound he had always enjoyed. He stepped out, pulled up his collar and began walking.

It was quiet outside and almost dark. The faint glow of streetlights reflected and trembled in the puddles. He wished he were going somewhere, somewhere where someone was waiting for him. It began to rain harder as he passed Mary's Dome, the cathedral. Although he had quickened his step with the increased rainfall, he stopped for a moment to look at its colossal size and grandeur through the downpour. Stone arches shone in their wetness. He suddenly shivered and desired immediate shelter. Perhaps he could sit inside for a while. Just until the rain stopped. Turning, he climbed the stone steps which led to massive wooden doors. Gingerly pressing down on a wrought-iron door-handle, he pushed. Creaking heavily, the door opened and Albert stepped inside.

The cathedral foyer was dark and smelled slightly musty. The door fell heavily into place behind him, the sound echoing and re-echoing. Hesitantly he walked on through the foyer into the lighted sanctuary. It was huge compared to that of his own church and, comparatively, quiet. People talked and whispered behind their hands when he and his mother walked in on Sunday mornings. They read bulletins and took out peppermints. But perhaps because there were so few people here there was no noise. He breathed in the quiet and relaxed.

There were three or four people present in the front pews, heads bowed and silent, praying, as far as he could tell. Albert stood for a moment and then slowly made his way toward the middle of the church, inconspicuously sliding onto a shining wooden bench. The pew was small - almost too small for his bulk. He grinned to himself. What would his mother say? Or his ward elder? Or Mr. DeVries, his employer and an avid commentator on all false churches?

After a while the quiet had embraced him to such a degree that he felt as if time had stopped. Did it matter to God whether you sat in a Reformed church or a Roman Catholic one? Of course it did, he knew that. But it was raining outside and the state of one's heart, was that not what God considered? He pulled out his handkerchief and wiped his face dry. If a church happened to be on your way in a rainstorm and that church was Roman Catholic, well then ... Well then, what? It certainly was peaceful here.

He cautiously examined the stained-glass windows on his right. Impressive and grand, the outside raindrops glowed with colour through the matted glass as they danced their way down. He shifted his frame somewhat and his foot knocked against a wooden slat beneath the pew in front of him. He contemplated the kneeling bench with interest. Padded with red leather, it appeared comfortable. He looked about again. There was no one around except the few worshipers at the front and the only one staring at him as he peered about was a statue of Mary in the aisle next to him. Clad in a sky-blue stone robe, she eyed him serenely. Cautiously he slid his knees onto the padded red leather and bowed his head.

'*Our Father ...*' He could not recall ever before having knelt for prayer in church. He did kneel for prayer when he went to bed. It is not a matter of knees or kneeling, the minister had told them in catechism, but a matter of the heart. And yet, kneeling always made his heart more submissive. Was it submissive now? So many thoughts – could you be submissive with so many thoughts running around in your head?

'*Hallowed be Thy name ...*' There was a strange smell here. It reminded him of ... What was it? Yes, Christmas when Mother brought out the candles. It was the scent of sweet tallow. Mary's statue, just ahead of him in the centre aisle, had a number of candles aglow in front of it. Several of them were smoking, were at the end of their wick. Luther had knelt in such churches and so had Calvin. But he was neither a Luther nor a Calvin. He ran his hand over the wood in front of him. The grain was smooth. Sometimes he was not even sure of the truth he stood for. Was the truth always smooth? He went to church, had gone to a Christian school, read the Bible at mealtimes and before he went to bed, prayed at set times and was able to recite a fair number of the catechism questions and answers. Did those matters encompass the truth? And if he heard a lie, would he be able to detect it? He sighed. All of life, all of life ... was it not one confrontation after another? Were simple problems not large ones in miniature? And each spoken word ... were you not judged for it?

'*Thy kingdom come ...*' Most times, he admitted to himself as he shifted his knees about on the red leather, he had no thoughts of God's kingdom at all. There were only the day-by-day affairs of coping with small things, of pleasing his mother and of doing his work properly for Mr. DeVries.

'Thy kingdom come ...' He moved his body back up onto the bench again and rubbed his knees. In heaven there would be no marriage. The statue of Mary smiled at him benignly. The Roman Catholics believed that she was immaculate, pure, undefiled; and that she had never had relations with her husband Joseph. The figure certainly seemed flawless. There was one thing he had never doubted about her – and that was that she surely must have loved her Son. But then, Jesus would have been easier to love than an Albert. Contemplating the statue, he began to whisper confidentially.

'I know that you were highly favoured, but you were human – you did have sin.'

Mary kept on smiling. A dozen candles shone brightly at her feet. He imagined lighting candles at his mother's feet, imploring her to intercede, begging her to help with some problem. Did candles have to be made of tallow? Did he not often light candles at his mother's feet in other ways? – by always deferring to her and conceding that she was right; by asking if he might do this or that; by permitting her to take a role that somehow made him weak and ineffective, even though it seemed to all the world that he was the provider and the man of the house. Tonight was actually the first time that he could remember that he had actually done something without asking her permission. He regarded the statue again. The sky-blue of the robe was peaceful and her eyes were pensive, as if she was thinking deeply. But there was a hair-line crack along the folds of her stone robe.

He knelt down again on the leather and rested his forehead against the pew in front of him. He did love his mother. Hadn't he taken care of her all these years? Perhaps, perhaps he just didn't like her. Did she love him? Had she reason to not love him? His forehead rubbed against the smooth wood and slipped just a bit as sweat trickled past his eyebrows. He could not recall that she had ever said, 'I love you, Albert.' There had been phrases like, 'I'm proud of you, Albert,' when he had graduated from college and if he donated money to the church or Christian school, she would say, 'The Lord loves a cheerful giver', but that was about as close as he could get.

A slight noise to his right startled him. He raised his head and saw a woman standing by Mary's statue. She fumbled with her purse and Albert watched her take out a wallet, and after taking a ten dollar bill out of it, fold it and deposit it into a slot. She then made the sign of the cross and lit two of the candles. Hunched down, her hands folded on top of the floor, he presumed that she was praying. Her blue raincoat dripped water onto the carpet making bright red spots. He watched her for a long time. She was motionless but he could see that her lips were moving. What petition, he wondered, was worth ten dollars? What question so burned her heart that she had to kneel down on a faded, red carpet in front of a statue? Had Eli watched Hannah in this manner? She rose and turned and he could see that there were tears in her eyes. Ashamed to be watching, he bowed his head down on the pew in front of him again.

'Excuse me. Could you tell me what time it is?'

He opened his eyes. The woman was standing by his side.

'I'm sorry to bother ... to bother you.'

She stuttered a bit and he pulled up his coat sleeve to look at his watch.

'That's all right. It's a quarter after nine.'

'Thank you.'

Her blue raincoat was still shiny with rain and black hair curled damply around an oval face. She was fairly young. He would guess her to be around twenty-four or five.

'Are you the ... the priest?'

She looked at him rather anxiously and he wondered if he had put on his collar backwards. The statue of Mary silhouetted behind her and compassion overcame him for her misplaced faith.

'The priest?'

'Yes ... he was to meet me at nine. I thought ... you ...?'

Clearly within the chambers of his mind he heard Peter's words, *'But you are a chosen people, a royal priesthood, a holy nation, a people belonging to God, that you may declare the praises of Him Who called you out of darkness into His wonderful light.'* The girl continued to stare at him. Her dark blue eyes were pensive and he smiled at them.

'I'm not the priest. That is to say, I'm not the priest you're looking for.'

'Oh, but you are a priest then?'

'Well ...'

He looked for words to explain to her that as a believer he reflected the glory of God and ... His thoughts got no further.

'If you're not busy, maybe you have time to speak to me for a moment?'

He saw the statue smiling behind her back and he smelled the tallow.

'I'm not Roman Catholic.'

For a moment looking into her dark hazel eyes, he was sorry he was not. The girl blinked and took a step backwards.

'You're not?'

He shook his head.

'No, I'm sorry if my being here misled you.'

'You were praying.'

She said it defensively. He felt a trifle foolish and stood up.

'I came in out of the rain. It's peaceful here. Yes, I was praying.'

'I'm not Roman Catholic either.'

She suddenly smiled up at him and he could see irregular white teeth.

'Oh?'

'If you were praying,' she was quite earnest again, 'then maybe you know about God ... about prayer?'

Albert Tenfold had led a very structured life. It had been drilled into him from childhood that organization and discipline were next to godliness. When he was growing up, his mother had always made sure that he had porridge for breakfast, drank milk with his lunch and went to bed at a set time after dinner. School was a given and catechism a must. There were always two services to attend every Sunday, regular young people's meetings, and occasional youth rallies. After confession of faith at age seventeen, he had tithed, celebrated the Lord's Supper every two months and attended study weekends on various Bible topics.

'About God ...?' he answered the girl slowly, 'About prayer?'

She nodded at him. During his entire thirty-five years of Christian living, Albert had never been confronted with questions of this sort by anyone outside of his church circle, and it hung in front of him like an unused banner. He played for time.

'Do you want to go for a coffee and talk for a while?'

She considered him for a long moment and he wondered if she felt that this cathedral was a safe place, a place were strangers could be approached without fear.

'I'd talk here but it's just that ...'

He stopped abruptly and made a small gesture towards the front pews. There were still some people there and Albert's whisper carried.

'Sure, I'll go for a coffee.'

Without another glance at the statue, she walked down the aisle ahead of him and he followed.

The rain had eased off considerably. There was a smell of sweetness in the air and in the distance a dog barked.

'What's your name?'

She asked the question almost as soon as they reached the pavement.

'Albert. What's yours?'

'Victoria – but my friends call me Vicky.'

He grinned.

'Why are you laughing?'

'Albert and Victoria.'

She looked at him blankly.

'You know,' he explained, 'they used to be the king and queen of England.'

She grinned too.

'Well, you might have the makings of a king but I'm not exactly a queen.'

He awkwardly offered her his arm as she gingerly edged past a puddle. He barely noted her touch. Out of the corner of his eye he saw that her hand was small with well-rounded, clean nails. He could not help but think of how his mother clung to him in this sort of weather, his mother who always wore gloves. Her voice bounced off the sidewalk now and he heard her voice clearly within the chambers of his mind. 'Your arm, Albert! Give me your arm!' He sighed and quickened his step. Vicky looked up at him questioningly.

'You probably have other things to do, right? Actually you don't ...'

He didn't let her finish.

'No, no. I'm sorry if I've given you the impression that ... that I'm not enjoying myself.'

He finished the sentence rather lamely and almost blushed.

The coffee shop was crowded and the noisy atmosphere fell about them like an intrusion. They stood in line for a while, not speaking, studying the pastry behind the glass.

'I'll pay for my own.'

She spoke curtly and avoided looking at him.

'No, please ...'

He didn't really know what to say but went on hesitatingly.

'I'd be honoured to pay for your coffee and ...'

'Maybe,' and she spoke in a low voice, 'maybe you won't be honoured after we talk.'

He felt unsure suddenly. Maybe this girl was a prostitute; maybe she had committed a murder; maybe ... He got no further with his thoughts.

'Can I help you, sir?'

'A glazed donut, please, and a coffee.'

'To go?'

'No, we'll eat here.'

Vicky ordered the same and allowed him to pay.

There was an empty table by the window. It had begun to rain again and the sound eased the tension between them.

Albert stirred his coffee and wondered how to begin the conversation. But he didn't have to.

'Do you still want me to talk to you?'

He looked at her. She was fingering her donut without eating it. Damp hair clung to her forehead.

'Yes, of course ... but if you'd rather not.'

His spoon splashed some coffee over the side of his cup and she reached for a napkin from the holder on the table.

'Oh, I'd like to talk to someone. Actually I have to talk to someone or ...'

She stopped and rubbed the brown puddle on the table fiercely, small fingers white with the pressure.

'Well,' he said, matter of factly, 'I'm at your service.'

She took a small sip of her coffee, smiled nervously at him and began.

'A year ago I was a student at the university here in town. I was enrolled in Political Studies ...'

She lifted her coffee with both hands and stared out the window. He waited. He didn't have to wait long. She no longer seemed to be speaking to him but, considering her reflection in the window, spoke to it.

'I resented most things ... rich people, styrofoam, male chauvinists, acid rain and apartheid. I joined Greenpeace, the Sierra Club and Amnesty International and talked about a lot of things without really understanding any of them. I said that I was an agnostic and I was flattered when I raised eyebrows.'

She paused for breath, put down her cup and crumbed off a piece of her donut. Not eating it, but turning it over in her hand, she went on.

'All my friends were saying the same sort of things. One of them ... one of them ...'

She picked up her coffee, sipped again and returned to her reflection in the window.

'To make a long story short ... I became pregnant ... the father was someone I hardly knew ... the baby was just another thing I didn't really understand.'

Albert had been watching her face. He had been listening to the sound of her voice thinking that it didn't really fit in the story. She had a child's voice and her hands were a child's hands.

'The group I hung around with all advised me to go for an abortion. So I did what was expected of me ... I scheduled an appointment for an abortion at a health clinic.'

Albert sat up straighter and took a bite out of his donut. His heartbeat increased and he felt sweat trickle down his armpits.

'But my friends ... they suggested that I try a new abortion technique ... It was some sort of drug. So I ... I looked into it. There was a special clinic and I ... I went to it.'

Some people passed their table and Vicky stopped talking. She gulped down some of her coffee and coughed. Albert cleared his throat. He racked his brain for Biblical texts - prayed for some homily to come to him which he might deliver here at this coffee shop which would relieve the tension and which would teach both error and compassion.

'I ... there was a staff ... and they ...'

Vicky seemed not to notice his discomfort. Engulfed in the past, her voice kept on confessing.

'... they examined me and had me sign two documents. One was a release form and one was a government something or other. Then a nurse came and she had this small suitcase. She explained things ... how this drug would work. I didn't understand it all but didn't let on. I was scared ...'

Albert took another bite of his donut. It tasted bland and he had trouble swallowing it.

'Was I sure I wanted to go ahead? That's what the nurse said. And I said, 'Yes ... yes, I was sure.' And then she opened the suitcase and gave me a small box. There were three pills in the box, just three little pills. She brought me a glass of water and then I ... I swallowed those pills. Just like that ...'

Her voice broke and Albert took a swallow of his coffee and cleared his throat again. Vicky pushed her donut towards the centre of the table and picked up her napkin.

'Sometimes you want to redo time, to relive just one moment. Have you ever had that?'

She turned her face to him fully for the first time and he noted that her eyes were hazel with small flecks of green in them. He answered slowly.

'I've had that. Yes, ... I've had that lots of times. It's because we continually do things that we regret later. We always ...'

'Yes,' she interrupted, 'but what if the thing you do is so ... '

She stopped again and then went on.

'The pills made me sick. I had cramps, nausea and diarrhoea and I bled ... I just bled and bled. I phoned the clinic and they told me not to worry but I felt so sick. I could barely get out of bed to the bathroom. There was so much pain and I couldn't see properly. I finally phoned an ambulance ... they came and took me to the hospital.'

'Did you ... had you ...'

Albert couldn't help it. He had to ask.

'Had you lost the baby?'

She stared at him with her hazel eyes.

'Lost it? You don't understand ... if you lose something ... well, then you can maybe find it later. I failed to abort with the pill but it had done the job. The child in me was dead and, as a result, I had to have a surgical abortion and ... and during that surgical abortion ... there was infection, a bad infection – and then I had a hysterectomy.'

'Oh.'

It was all Albert could say. He played with his cup and noted that it had stopped raining again. Was this what she had said to Mary? Was this what her silent lips had been speaking of to a mere statue? Had she lit a candle to atone for murder? He shivered.

'They didn't tell me that I'd feel such guilt. No one ever mentioned the fact that I would feel such a ...'

She stopped and tried again.

'No one explained ... you see, I know for a fact that it was a child ... not just a nothing ... and I killed this child ... my child. My friends laughed at me when I tried to explain how I felt ... and I was so lost.'

'Your family ...'

Albert got no further than two words. She laughed.

'I have no family. That is, my mother died when I was seven and my father is living with wife number four. I haven't been home for years and don't plan to go there now.'

'Oh.'

Again it was all Albert was able to say. How would his mother react to a Vicky? 'Mother, may I introduce you to Vicky. She just had an abortion and is feeling a little down.'

'I ... I realize that whatever it was that I was trying to be last year and before that, was a fraud – was not real. But there is something real ... there has to be ... and I'm trying to find it. So I wanted to ask the priest about God and then he wasn't there. But you were.'

Albert was suddenly calm.

'You see,' she went on, staring out the window again, 'if there is nothing, then I wouldn't be able to live. I ... I ... I don't know if you understand, but I have to be able to apologize to someone for ... for killing this baby.'

There was a sudden clap of thunder outside and the rain began again. It was a steady rain, thick drops splattering the sidewalk. Vicky shivered. Albert began to speak. Cautiously his voice crept across the table.

'I think I understand what you mean,' he said. 'Can I tell you something about myself? Something I haven't told ... something I have never told anyone?'

He stopped. She turned her eyes towards him. He could read neither approval nor disapproval in them.

'Sure.'

Her passionate voice had become a flat – gone bland, disappointed perhaps. Maybe she wanted a quick answer. But he wouldn't be able to answer quickly. He looked at her steadily.

'It isn't easy for me to speak actually. I'm more of a doer than a speaker.'

She didn't respond and he went on hesitantly, choosing his words with care.

'I was born during the first year of the Second World War. We lived in a small village somewhere in the north of Holland. I don't remember much.'

His hands crumpled the napkin he was holding.

'Its funny, the things that I do remember though. Things like the creaking of the cradle I must have slept in – things like a horse pulling a milk cart passing our house every morning. My mother says that my first word was horse.'

He looked at her, waiting for some sort of response but there was none. And his intuition told him that she wasn't really listening because the words meant nothing to her, nothing at all. But he went on all the same.

'My father had a good job. He was a lawyer – a very good lawyer, my mother tells me. He had a lot of business and people liked him very much. When the war came, he helped people. He helped Jews in particular. The strange thing is that I don't remember my father's face but I do remember that he was tall – very tall. Perhaps I remember that because he used to throw me up into the air and catch me in his arms.'

Vicky was still not reacting to his story at all. If anything, she was slightly uncomfortable. But Albert persisted in talking.

'In the first years of the war my father lived at home. He was not suspected by the Germans of any subterfuge even though he was involved in the underground. His speciality had something to do with illegal documents. But later on he had to leave our house and go into hiding. My mother and I only saw him on those few occasions that he deemed it was safe to come for a short visit. On one of those visits the Gestapo must have been tipped off because shortly after he arrived they surrounded our house. My mother was frantic and hid my father behind a secret panel in the living room. When the Gestapo came into the house a moment later, she and I were in the kitchen. They didn't ask where he was but simply began searching ...'

Albert stopped and stretched his legs under the table. He wasn't looking for a reaction in Vicky's eyes anymore. He had actually almost forgotten she was there.

'And then ... what happened then?'

Her voice called him back and he saw that she was genuinely interested.

'Then? Well miracle of miracles, they didn't find him.'

He stopped and stretched his legs again.

'What was the point of telling me the story?'

'The point? I'm still coming to that. You see, after their search one of the officers hunched down by me, small boy of three that I was, and began to play with me. He had a chocolate bar in his pocket and even though my mother frowned, I took it when he gave it to me. He helped me unwrap the candy and I began to eat ... and all the while my mother was glaring. But it tasted wonderfully good and the man seemed so friendly.

When he took me on his lap a moment later, I completely ignored my mother and smiled at him. He joked with me and then asked if maybe my father was playing hide and seek. I laughed out loud, greatly amused that he would ask such a question. He laughed too and asked where my father, who must be very clever indeed, was hiding.

I slid off his lap, walked into the living room, and stood by the panel. When they discovered my father a few moments later, I remember that I did not feel quite right about it but didn't really know why. I ran to my mother for comfort but she spat in my face.

Then they ... they took him out into our yard and shot him, right in front of the house. The soldier who had given me the chocolate said, 'Danke schön', bowed to my mother and myself and left. He was mocking us. Then my mother made me go out to look at the dead body of my father ... and I screamed and screamed until the neighbours came and took me away.'

'You didn't mean it,' Vicky said. 'You didn't know what you were doing. You were only a little child.'

'Yes,' Albert answered thickly, 'you are right. I was only a child.'

The thunder rolled in the distance and Vicky's eyes were compassionate.

'How did you manage? What did your mother ...?'

'She ... I lived with the neighbours until the end of the war. She didn't want ... me.'

'Oh.'

She drummed her fingers along the table edge and regarded him seriously.

'You were praying in church. You told me that you were praying. So, what did you do with your guilt? Or didn't you pray when you were little? Or what I'm trying to say is how did you deal with the fact that you caused ...'

He smiled at her. The fact that he now felt forgiven for the death he had caused did not make it easier to speak of at this time.

'No one really spoke to me about my father's death. The neighbours were very kind. But as I grew older I felt, also because of what other children said to me at school, that I was solely responsible for the fact that my mother was a widow. When my mother remarried in 1946 I had been living with her again for about a year and my stepfather made plans to emigrate to Canada. We never spoke of my own father. As I grew older my mind told me that I had only been an irresponsible child during the war, but my heart accused me of murder every day. We went to church, yes, and we read the Bible.'

Vicky's eyes were wide with sympathy. He went on.

'What finally saved me from this terrible guilt feeling, Vicky, was the fact that God allowed me to see that He was totally in control of all things.'

He was quiet and for a moment saw himself earlier that evening, kneeling in the pew. He had been thinking about truth – well, this was the truth – God's control over one's life, God's tender, loving control, always drawing His own to Himself with cords He wove throughout every day life. Vicky continued to look at him and he went on.

'God was in control of my father's life. He had stipulated when and where my father would die. And, I was also led to see that, but for my father's death, I would not have been as drawn to study the Bible so thoroughly; to investigate the mighty God I worship; to understand that He is a God Who forgives when we are sorry.'

Vicky stared at him unblinkingly. He wondered if she had understood what he was saying.

'I think that if you are looking for God, Vicky,' he finally ended, 'it's safe to say that He is making you look; that He has used this very tragic thing that has happened to you – this abortion – to make you look for Him.'

A waitress stopped by their table.

'How is everything with you folks? Anything else you need?'

'No, thank you.'

Albert was quick to answer but then amended, 'Maybe you would like some more coffee, Vicky?'

'No, no thank you.'

Her voice was thin and lifeless. The tables around them were almost empty. The waitress smiled.

'All right. We'll be closing soon. It's after eleven.'

Albert glanced at his watch. He imagined that his mother would be livid by now. He took out the small notepad and pen he kept in his pocket and jotted down his church address.

'I can't give you faith, Vicky. I can't give you forgiveness either. But I can tell you where to look for it.'

'I know God is there.'

Vicky whispered the words, paused and then went on.

'I know ... but I don't know how I know.'

'Do you have a Bible?'

'Yes, I bought one last week.'

'Then you must read it every day.'

The lights dimmed and they automatically stood up. The rain had let up again.

'I'll walk you home.'

'No, no ... I live very close by.'

'Well, then it shouldn't be a problem.'

'No, no ... please, I need time to think and be by myself. Thanks.'

The waitress eyed them impatiently as they walked past her to the door.

'Thanks again, Albert.'

'Goodbye, Vicky.'

He watched her walk away, small and slight in a coat the colour of her eyes, and felt some pain.

In the elevator ride up to the fifth floor, Albert rehearsed what he would say when he walked in. There was no doubt in his mind that his mother would still be awake.

'Albert?!'

'Yes, Mother.'

'Where were you all evening?'

'Out with a girl, Mother. She'd had an abortion and felt rather miserable. So I took her to a coffee shop and tried to tell her about the forgiveness we can have in Christ.'

He contemplated the elevator buttons and continued his conversation.

'Do you know about forgiveness, Mother? You don't, do you?'

'Albert, what kind of way is that to speak to your mother?'

'Sorry, but I had to say it sooner or later. Even though God forgave me for inadvertently causing father's death you never did. You never let me forget that I was the one who ...'

The elevator had reached the fifth floor. The hall was quiet and Albert's inward voice dissolved.

He took out his keys as he walked towards the apartment. They jangled and he stifled a yawn, hoping against hope that his mother would, after all, be asleep. The door was silent but before he could fit the key into the lock, it opened. Mrs. Dorman stared up at him.

'Albert, you're finally home.'

'Yes, but what are you still doing here, Mrs. Dorman?'

'Your mother, Albert ... it's your mother.'

'What about my mother? What's the matter with her?'

They were still standing at the open door and he moved past the small, dark woman into the apartment.

'Maybe you should sit down before ...'

'What's the matter with my mother, Mrs. Dorman?'

'She felt ill, Albert. She had a pain in her chest. So I called an ambulance ...'

'Yes?'

A strange feeling came over him.

'They came within five minutes of my calling and the attendant said that it was her heart ...'

He stared at Mrs. Dorman. The woman was nervously twisting her hands together.

'It was a heart attack, Albert. I rode in the ambulance with her to the hospital. They took her to intensive care. But before they took her there I promised that I would come back to the apartment and wait for you.'

'Thank you, Mrs. Dorman. That was kind of you.'

'Are you going down to the hospital now?'

She looked at him, her eyes wide and helpless. His mother was her best friend.

'Yes, I will and I'll phone you in the morning to let you know how things are.'

'Thank you, Albert. Thank you.'

She walked towards the door and then turned.

'Wasn't it too bad that you were out just tonight of all nights?'

'Yes. Goodnight, Mrs. Dorman.'

After he closed the door behind her, Albert walked into the living room. A just-begun Scrabble game lay on the table. The words 'apple', 'tax' and 'problem' stared up at him – three words made by his mother and Mrs. Dorman. He ran his fingers through the word 'problem' and then tilted the board, emptying the letters into the Scrabble box. Maybe his mother had already felt ill when he had left. She had looked just a bit off colour. He closed the box and sighed. A great weariness crept over him. But greater than the weariness was the feeling that he had failed somewhere – again. He sat down and cupped his face with his hands. If he was really honest with himself he had to admit that he had no great affection for his mother. *'Honour your father and mother - which is the first commandment with a promise - that it may go well with you and that you may enjoy long life on the earth.'* He didn't really know at this precise moment whether or not he had honoured his mother. Holding him with invisible ropes as it were, she had made him aware of the past in innumerable ways. The small clearing of her throat when the minister read the sixth commandment, had always made him edgy and nervous as a child – not because God had not forgiven him, but because she had not. He sighed again and slowly stood up. Better go to the hospital and see how things were.

It was still raining when he drove his car through the streets not five minutes later. The windshield wipers beat a soft rhythm and the quiet of the hour calmed him. He could not stop thinking about his mother's life. She had been happy, as far as he could tell, with his stepfather. His stepfather had been a good husband, kind, gentle and hard-working. But his mother had always been reserved, had always held back. Albert could not remember that he had ever seen her kiss his stepfather, or himself for that matter. He could not remember either, that she had ever sung spontaneously or laughed genuinely at something silly. On the other hand, she had always cooked good meals, had provided adequate clothing and had kept the house very neat. She had led an ordered existence that would maybe now, he went on to think, come to an end. What could he say to her as she lay on her hospital bed? If he could never speak to her again but this one time, what should he say to this woman who had born him in her belly for nine months and who must, it seemed to him, have cultivated some love for him? But he could not feel the love as he sat in the car and drove through the dark.

The streets were deserted but he stopped punctually at every red light, playing for time, having no particular desire to get to the hospital quickly. He thought of Vicky – a compassionate, young woman who had wept because she had killed her unborn child. Perhaps Vicky had more compassion for her dead child than his mother had ever had for her him. No, that was a ridiculous thought, an unfair thought. He should not be unfair. What was it he had said to Vicky? Nothing, he had said, nothing is outside of God's control. God had used the tragedy in his life to make him realize just how dependent he was on God. What was it the minister had preached on last Sunday? Oh, yes, forget what is behind and strain toward the goal for which God has called us. Another red light – he brought the car to a slow stop. His mother had been unable to forget what lay behind her. They had never really talked about his father and what had happened – never. Would they be able to talk about it now? If they talked about it, would she be able to forget – to forgive? Had it hampered her road to heaven? He should have talked to her. The light turned green. He stepped on the gas and began to drive faster. Was it not also true that, if she had harboured a grudge against him all these years, he had also harboured a grudge against her? He drove through the next red light.

The hospital entrance was quiet. The glass doors opened silently under his push.

'Can I help you, sir?'

The nurse at the desk looked efficient.

'My mother was admitted earlier this evening – a heart attack. I've only just heard and now ...'

'What's your mother's name?'

'Tenfold'.

She consulted her book and peered up at him from her swivel chair.

'She's in intensive care, sir. Fourth floor. You'll have to ask at the desk there.'

'Thank you.'

He walked on towards the elevator.

The fourth floor corridor had a red carpet – red, the colour of blood. He walked over it quickly and with some trepidation. There were two nurses at the desk. They both looked up at him and smiled.

'Yes?'

'My mother was admitted earlier this evening with a heart attack. I understand she's in intensive care.'

He eyed the double doors behind their desk to the intensive care unit with some degree of dislike. They appeared so grim, grey and dismal – as if they only let in and not out.

'Your mother's name, sir?'

'Tenfold.' He spoke with some impatience.

'Tenfold?'

'Yes.'

There was some hesitation on the nurses' part before one of them responded rather sympathetically.

'Could you wait in the waiting room, sir? I'll ring for the doctor on call to speak with you.'

'The doctor?'

He spoke cautiously, feeling his way over the word.

'Why must I speak with the doctor? I just want to ...'

'He'll be with you directly. You can sit down over there, sir.'

They both indicated a small lounge behind the desk and smiled at him.

'All right.'

He walked towards the lounge, shuffling his feet on the red carpet, uncomfortably aware that both nurses were eyeing him behind his back. There were three brown chairs and a leather couch. Indecisively he stood for a moment and then sat down heavily in one of the chairs. The table sported magazines – colourful editions featuring smiling men and ladies. The clock on the wall told him it was 12:01. He picked up a magazine and then laid it back down.

'Mr. Tenfold?'

A young man stood at the entrance of the lounge. Albert stood up.

'Please be seated. I'd just like to speak with you a moment.'

'My mother ...'

Albert was afraid to phrase the question. The young man came closer and offered his hand.

'I'm Doctor Ellis.'

'Albert Tenfold.'

They both sat down and Albert waited.

'Your mother was admitted around nine o'clock this evening. I happened to be on duty and so I attended her.'

'It was a heart attack?'

Albert began searching out the pieces of the puzzle that lay between him and a finished picture – pieces that the doctor held.

'Yes,' Dr. Ellis nodded and then asked, 'You live in town?'

'I live at home with my mother. I was not there tonight when she became ill.'

Albert's voice was meticulous and short.

'Ah.'

'My mother ...' Albert began again.

'Yes, your mother did have a heart attack.'

It was now 12:05. The clock, Albert thought, seemed to move faster than this young man.

'How is my mother?'

Dr. Ellis reached out a thin and long hand and placed it on Albert's knee.

'I'm sorry, Mr. Tenfold. Your mother passed away about an hour ago.'

Albert sat very still. The doctor removed his hand.

'Is there something I can get for you – a coffee? ...'

'No, no, thank you.'

'It may sound callous Mr. Tenfold, but perhaps it was a blessing. You see, it was a massive heart attack. There had been extensive damage - several organs were not functioning any more ...'

'May I see her? May I see the body?'

The room was very quiet. The doctor had offered to come in with Albert but he had refused saying that he wanted to be alone. The door fell shut behind him and he stood leaning against it for several moments, breathing in the nothing odour of the room. He looked at the white sheets and saw that his mother's form scarcely made a dint in the bed. For a moment he thought he saw the sheets moving, as if his mother was breathing. But it was a trick of the eyes, because when he moved closer there was only stillness – unbroken stillness.

He stood at the foot of the bed and held onto the railing.

'Hello, Mother.'

Moving to the side, he pulled up a chair and sat down.

'I've been gone most of the evening, I know,' he said, 'but I didn't know. I really had no idea that you would die tonight.'

She didn't answer and he looked down at his hands.

'You know,' he went on, looking up again, 'I thought that I might get a chance to talk to you tonight about the past. As I drove down in the car I was thinking about all the things that I wanted to say to you. And now it's too late.'

He stopped and pulled his chair a little closer to the bed.

'But maybe it's not too late – not too late for me. You see,' and he looked up again at her dead form, 'you see, maybe if I had brought it up, maybe if I had told you that I was sorry, the way I told God that I was sorry, you might have forgiven me. Now you died without forgiving me.'

His voice caught and he lay his head on the edge of the bed's steel railing. But the words flowed on, the words tumbled out past all the years of stifle, hitting the floor with their vehemence.

'But maybe this evening you did forgive me. Before you died, perhaps you thought, ah, I should have told my son that I love him. I should have ...'

His voice broke again and still he went on.

'I do not know what you did or thought in those last moments. I cannot judge that. God will judge that ... and this is what I want to say to God and to you – I forgive you, mother. I forgive you for haunting me, for never allowing me to have my own life outside of yours'

He wiped his face with the back of his sleeve,

' ... and yet it was my own fault too. Because I let you do it and I could have stopped it.'

He stood up and regarded her face. Smooth and unperturbed, she lay silently. It was almost as if she would open her eyes in a second and say, 'Albert, is the tea ready yet?'

'No - no tea, Mother,' he whispered, 'but perhaps milk and honey - perhaps that.'

Then he left the room, not even turning for a last look at the door.

* * *

Three days later there was a funeral. Although Albert accepted many condolences at the funeral home, he was not quite comfortable with the 'I'm sorry about your mother ...' remarks. But was it necessary, he reflected, as he sat in the left front pew, flanked only by three church members whom he had asked to be pallbearers, that others knew how he felt? Was it necessary that someone understood? The minister read from John, unperturbed by Albert's thoughts.

'When Martha heard that Jesus was coming, she went out to meet him, but Mary stayed at home. *'Lord,' Martha said to*

Jesus, 'if you had been here, my brother would not have died.' But I know that even now ...'

There was no clock in the sanctuary. The coffin stood directly beneath the pulpit. His mother had always sat in the ninth row from the front. Albert turned his head slightly and almost expected to see her there, smartly dressed in her green summer coat, straight and dignified with her eyes on the minister. There were a lot of people behind him and his gaze passed over them impersonally, passed over them and then suddenly stopped. In the exact place where his mother had been wont to sit, was a slight figure in a blue raincoat.

'"If you had been here," Martha said to Jesus, "my brother would not have died."'

The minister's voice rose and fell about him.

'These words of Martha tell us a lot about what she was actually thinking. She was thinking, if you had been here, and you could have been because we sent you a message, then you could have prevented Lazarus' death.'

Albert turned again and saw that Vicky's face was turned towards the pulpit with studious attention. Why would Vicky be here? He'd given her the address of the church, of course. But it wasn't Sunday and ...

'Jesus' direct statement, "Your brother will rise again", evoked an earthly response from Martha. "Yes, I know that he will rise again on the last day."'

Albert eyed the coffin again. His mother would rise again – the lid of the coffin would open and she would climb out, maybe jump out.

'Martha wanted an immediate resurrection - she wanted a "now" answer, brothers and sisters. We all often want a "now" answer and we forget that God has His own agenda - His own way of working things out for good.'

Albert shifted his feet and listened – listened with his own ears and also with Vicky's.

'I am the resurrection and the life. He who believes in Me will live, even though he dies; and whoever lives and believes in Me will never die. Do you believe this?'

A shaft of sunlight fell through the window at the right and a pool of brightness bathed the front section of the church.

'The question is not, brothers and sisters, whether Martha believed Jesus' words – the question is, do you believe them?'

He walked out behind the minister. The pallbearers walked with him and the people from the funeral home pushed the coffin sedately ahead of them all towards the door and on to the parking lot. The small figure in the blue raincoat reached his side before he reached the hearse.

'Albert! Albert! Wait!'

Scores of heads turned – turned and listened.

'It's been three days and I've been reading and looking. I just wanted you to know.'

The pallbearers had stopped walking and Albert smiled broadly before he went on to bury his mother.

'For while we were still weak,
at the right time Christ died for the ungodly.
For one will scarcely die for a righteous person -
though perhaps for a good person
one would dare even to die -
but God shows his love for us
that while we were still sinners,
Christ died for us.'
Romans 5:6-8

THE GIFT

It was when I was about four years old that I had my first dealings with Gertie and Harmen Maritaans. Harmen Maritaans was a farmer, and he asked if my father, who was a farmer's son turned cobbler and who did not always have enough work, would hire out to him a few days a week. I suppose they agreed upon a wage. Anyway, the upshot of it was that he went to the Maritaans' farm every Wednesday and Saturday – went there and took me along. I was a big, strapping lad, even for my four years and my father thought to instil in me a working ethic before I began school. He made me a small hoe, and my mother, doing her part, fashioned me a cover-all of sorts. Proud as a peacock I strutted behind my father that first day, hoe hanging nonchalantly over my bony, right shoulder.

'What have we here?' Harmen laughingly asked when he saw me.

Laughed a bit in an irritated manner, I think, for he thought I would be in the way. But I had been schooled well by my parents. Speak only when spoken to – be polite – do as you're told – and stay close to Father. I was father's shadow the initial weeks and when Harmen noted that I was actually useful, he accepted me as part of the deal, even gave me a penny at the close of the third week. Sometimes Gertie invited me into the kitchen, putting me in a chair by the big table and setting a steaming cup of milk flavoured with anise in front of me. She hugely enjoyed my contented slurping and before she sent me off back to my father, there was always a large slab of home-made bread with thickly spread butter and golden cheese. She usually made me eat it before going out. Instinctively I understood Harmen was not to see me receive the food so I would bolt down the bread as quickly as a puppy.

They had been married more than twenty years – Harmen and Gertie – twenty childless years. My mother used to say that it was a shame that they had no children because Gertie often looked very lonely. I was my parents' only child, but I was enough, my mother said, usually adding with a twinkle in her eyes, 'more than enough', and then she would hug me.

One Saturday morning, as I was playing in the milk-house behind the cooler, I overheard Gertie speaking to Harmen. Truth be told, I had been sent by father to fetch a pail but had sat down next to it to play with a kitten. Gertie had walked in after I had wasted some fifteen minutes or more in the milk-house and began scouring the cooler. She hadn't seen me on the cement floor on the other side of the cooler, and I had been about to stand up and disclose myself to her when the door opened again and Harmen entered as well. Before I could decide a safe course of action, Gertie's voice drifted over my head.

'I might be in the family way, Harmen.'

Her statement, though hesitant, stressed the 'might be'. I could see her legs from where I was sitting on the other side of the cooler. Her stockings were black and her skirt moved slightly as she methodically kept scouring as she spoke. Harmen was passing through the milk-house on his way to the barn. The kitten on my lap began to purr. I could see Harmen's feet as they slowed down at Gertie's words – slowed down some but did not stop. I wondered if he was looking at Gertie and although the urge was great, I did not peek. Harmen's feet kept moving towards the barn door. He opened it, walked through, and closed it behind him without saying a word in response to Gertie's revelation. Slightly uncomfortable, I stayed put. For a few minutes Gertie kept scouring as if her life depended on it. But then I heard and saw her brush drop to the ground. It fell rather close to me and I held my breath. But she did not bend over to pick it up. Her black stockings moved towards the outside door. It opened and swallowed her up as if she had not been there at all. Putting down the kitten, I stood up, stretched my stiff legs and followed Harmen into the barn.

My eyes had to adjust to the darker barn. I peered around for my father but did not see him although I could hear Harmen muttering as he was attending to the business of cleaning out the gutters. Slowly edging my way through the adjacent aisle past him, I made for the loft where I supposed father might have gone.

'"Might be" are wind words,' Harmen said, either to himself or to one of the cows, 'words that can take your breath away and words that can make you lose your footing.'

I could see Harmen between the cows. He had his back towards me and had stopped cleaning the gutters to stroke the belly of a cow who was due to calve shortly.

'No "might be" about you, girl,' he said and laughed briefly, 'But Gertie's not a cow. No, she's my wife and I love her.'

He leaned on his rake and waxed lyrical. I stopped short and hid behind a heifer, for fear that he might turn and see me and be upset by my listening to his soliloquy.

'The "might be's" that were yesterday not only knocked the wind out of Gertie, they laid her flat and crippled her for some time. So it's best that I not respond.'

He stood up straight and began to rake again, still talking as he raked. 'Sweep the words away,' he said, as the muck flew into the gutters, 'get them clean out of your heart before you go in to lunch. Chances are she's forgotten them herself by that time.'

I cautiously continued my walk and reached the steps to the loft. Climbing up I still could not find father but determined to stay put until Gertie rang the dinner bell. At that time, it turned out, that Father had been sent away by Harmen to deliver a load of hay to a distant neighbour. So it was just Harmen, Gertie and I who sat down for the midday meal.

Gertie's name was actually Gerda. She was German and Harmen had met her when he was in Berlin prior to World War I. He rescued her from a burning house, so the story went, and had married her shortly afterwards. I liked Gertie. She was always kind to me, but the truth was that most of the villagers kept their distance even though her Dutch was almost flawless and without accent.

After prayer, for which Harmen took off his cap covering his face with it, Gertie stood up and filled our bowls with home-made soup. She made thick, wonderful soup, and the chunks of sausage drifting about in it made my mouth water. Gertie was a good cook. She was usually quiet during mealtimes, but on that day she served both soup and conversation.

'There was a peddler at the door early this morning,' she said, before Harmen could get the first steaming spoonful of broth into his mouth, 'and he told me ...'

'Told you what?'

Harmen interrupted almost rudely and I could see, as I was blowing onto my spoon, that he was suspicious.

'That I was ... that is to say, ... that I looked ...'

Here she faltered, put down the ladle which she was still holding back into the soup tureen, and sat down. Harmen put down his spoon.

'You don't mean to tell me that a total stranger, and a peddler at that, told you ...'

He stopped, picked up his spoon again, filled it with soup and put it into his mouth without blowing on it to cool it down. That was a mistake. Scalding his tongue and choking, he coughed and sputtered for a full minute.

'You don't like peddlers,' Gertie stated flatly when he was done, her eyes on the soup pan.

I think they had forgotten me.

'That has nothing to do with it,' Harmen replied, again putting down his spoon in an agitated manner before he continued, 'Gert, you know we've been through this before. We've talked and talked and then some, and I thought that we had settled on leaving the matter alone. You can't harvest,' he added after a moment's silence, in which Gertie fixed her gaze on the blue-flowered wallpaper, 'you can't harvest a crop ...'

'Don't,' his wife interrupted, 'I'm not one of the fields around the farm here – I'm not a barren, rocky plot of soil that you ...'

She halted and I could see Harmen wondering if she was done or if he could safely resume eating his soup.

'Gertie,' he said softly, reaching for her hand across the table by way of reconciliation, and again, 'Gertie.'

'Oh, Harmen,' she whispered, 'Strange as it may sound to you, the man seemed to know. He said come spring ...'

She bit her lip and he sighed.

'Did he sell you anything?'

'Nein, no,' she answered, slipping into German for just one moment while running her fingers over the blue vinyl oilcloth on the table, 'No, he didn't. He had a backpack, but he never bothered to show me what was in it. Simply asked for a drink and after I offered him some bread as well as a bed for the night, should he need it, he sort of looked at me and said, 'Come spring, Gerda, come spring you'll be feeding more than the odd peddler who comes your way.' He didn't say I was expecting, Harmen, but that's what he meant. I just know it.

And when I went inside to cut him a slice of bread, he left. Because he was gone when I came out with it a few minutes later.'

'Gone?'

'Yes, gone and I could see neither hide nor hair of him down the road.'

'Maybe he snuck around the house and got into the barn for a nap,' Harmen wryly commented.

'Now, why would he do that when I had made it plain to him that I would put him up for the night?'

Harmen shrugged and picked up his spoon for the third time. I had almost finished my bowl.

'And he knew my name,' Gertie continued slowly, '... my real name, Harmen. And what do you say about that?'

But Harmen was deep into his lukewarm soup, sopping up some home-made bread, and she knew he wouldn't respond anymore.

In the evening, when mother tucked me into bed, I told her these things. Mother clucked and clucked some more and told me to be very kind to Gertie for she was sure that Gertie was apt to be quite sad for a while. But the truth of it was that mother and Harmen were both wrong. During the winter, Gertie's breasts grew fuller and her stomach began to extend like a little red cabbage. Harmen tended to smile more. And I know they both wept when Elizabeth was born. I know that because it was a Saturday morning and I was there at the farm that day. They wept when the child first wept and I was even allowed to look into the home-made wooden cradle that afternoon, marvelling at the tiny bundle of lungs and red hair that graced the flat embroidered sheets.

Harmen and Gertie Maritaans were not regular church-goers. Nominal Christians, they warmed pews at weddings, funerals and feast days, and perhaps the odd Sundays when both of them wanted to stretch their legs. The church was in the village some forty-five minutes from their farm. My father was an elder and I ascertained from listening in bed to a conversation between him and Mother that Rev. Kruimel was a bit hesitant about performing the baptism. But, as Father told Mother over a cup of hot chocolate as they sat in the kitchen before going to bed, the church elders had reminded Rev. Kruimel that Harmen and Gertie were generous to a fault about tithing and that they might possibly attend services more often now that they had a child.

'I don't know,' was all Mother would say and after a moment she added, 'I pray they will do so.'

'Rev. Kruimel is going to visit them soon,' Father said.

'He's very young,' Mother responded, 'do you yourself never ...'

She let her unfinished statement hang in the air, but the meaning was clear and I knew the answer to her question. No, Father never did. He was too much the hired man and too little the elder. He knew how to say 'yes, Harmen' and 'no, Harmen', but the only thing that was ever discussed at the Maritaans was crops and weather.

I saw Rev. Kruimel bicycle his way along the rather ill-kept road that led to the farm as I was hoeing the vegetable garden for Gertie one Saturday morning. Caught off-guard by a rabbit jumping out from behind a bush, his front wheel hit a pot-hole and he took a rather nasty fall. I dropped my hoe and ran over as fast as my legs could carry me.

'Are you all right?'

Sitting up slowly, Rev. Kruimel ran his right hand across his forehead and ruefully contemplated a small tear in the knee of his black trousers. Next to him his bicycle lay prostrate. I extended my hand.

'Well, young Matteus VanderSloot,' he smiled, 'good to see you.'

I said nothing but helped him stand up and watched as he dusted himself off.

'Lots of cracks and bumps in this road. Not enough rain, I expect,' Rev. Kruimel went on, 'Well, I haven't broken anything, except for my pride.'

'Are you going to visit the Maritaans, sir?' I asked, knowing it was an obvious truth, but at a loss as to what else to say.

'Yes, I am. I expect you know them quite well, Matteus?'

'Oh, yes, sir. I work here just like my father.'

I put my thumbs in the bib of my overalls, just as Harmen often did when he surveyed a field, and rocked on my heels.

'Well then, perhaps you can show me the way to the door.'

I was more than happy to do this, and running back to get my hoe, I was soon walking along Rev. Kruimel's side as he made his way up the rest of the lane holding onto the bicycle's handlebars.

Some ten minutes later we were both sitting at the kitchen table watching Gertie as she dandled the baby on her lap. The child had a fuzz of red blond hair crowning her little scalp and she gazed at her mother's dark blue eyes. Gertie was seemingly lost in the spell of motherhood and paid scant attention to either myself or Rev. Kruimel after she had poured him a cup of tea.

'Is Harmen in the barn?'

She nodded at the Reverend's question, then sighed and carried the baby to the cradle positioned near the stove.

'Can you rock her, Matteus?'

I was delighted to oblige. Rocking a cradle was much preferred in my mind to hoeing vegetables. The baby fascinated me and she fixed her great eyes on me as I gently moved the cradle back and forth. Gertie sat down across from Rev. Kruimel and clasped her two sturdy hands together in her lap. Save for the steady creaking of the wooden cradle, it was quiet in the room. Rev. Kruimel, who presumably knew that the Maritaans were notorious for their lack of speech, began again.

'Elizabeth is quite a miracle, isn't she?'

Gertie's gaze inadvertently stole back to the cradle and I rocked devotedly.

'That she is.'

The quiet descended again for a full minute and the clock ticked and ticked. Rev. Kruimel was also, I ascertained, a man of few words, except when he was preaching.

'Had you a reason for naming her Elizabeth?'

'Elizabeth was my mother-in-law's name. Harmen thought it fitting.'

'Indeed.'

And the clock ticked some more. Rev. Kruimel coughed, sipped some tea to help him and stood up. Gertie, evidently presuming that he was leaving, stood up as well and had his coat ready before he had time to say 'boo'. He accepted it but I knew he was startled at the quick termination of his call.

'I was just going over to see baby Elizabeth,' he said.

'We'll be calling her Liesl,' Gertie replied, and the way she pronounced 'Liesl' was like a caress.

'Liesl's a fine name, Corrie.'

I winced.

'Gerda. My name's Gerda.'

I had never heard her use her German name before.

'I'm sorry.'

Rev. Kruimel flushed as he spoke. Gertie's mouth softened into a smile as she reached the cradle.

'One of my sisters was a Liesl as well. She ... she died during the war and I'm ... that is, we ...'

She stopped. They both peered at the child. Liesl, almost as if she knew she had an audience, smiled a beatific smile. I ceased rocking. Gertie, after basking in the grandeur of that smile for a moment, told me to go back to my hoeing.

'Strange fellow, that Kruimel,' Gertie said to Harmen during the noon meal, while she was dishing out meat and potatoes.

'How so?' answered Harmen, after he had chewed on a tough piece of cartilage for a full minute.

'Well, he never mentioned God,' Gertie replied, 'not once. And he was here for a full thirty minutes. I clocked him.'

'That so.' Harmen took another bite.

'Yes.'

Gertie mashed her potatoes to a pulp with her fork before she went on.

'I can't imagine you not talking cows and soil when you're with another farmer.'

'But maybe,' Harmen answered, as he took a swallow of tea, 'maybe you're not part of the herd to him?'

'Ah,' said Gertie, 'I wonder.'

And then Liesl stirred and she got up to feed her, but as she bent over the cradle to pick up the child, she threw Harmen another fact over her shoulder.

'Truth is that he didn't even know my name.'

Although Father kept working at the Maritaans, my hours there dwindled radically once I began to attend school. When I did come, Gertie would often put Liesl in my charge and I played with her. Sometimes I carried her to the apple tree where Harmen had fashioned a small swing; other times I would carry her about on my back, pretending to be a horse; and still other times we would play hide and seek. She was as dear to me as the little sister I never had. Church-going was still a sporadic affair for Harmen and Gertie and I worried out loud to Mother one night that Liesl would not learn much about God – not the way I presumed she ought to learn. Mother was quiet for a while before she spoke.

'Have you prayed about it, Matteus?' she asked me then.

Ashamed I had to confess that I had not.

'I have an idea,' she said, 'What if you were to give Liesl your story Bible? What do you think about that?'

'My story Bible?' I repeated and then added, 'but Liesl can't read. She's too little.'

It was a story Bible my Oma had given me and although I was all of ten now and had most of the stories memorized, I still loved looking at the illustrations.

'Yes,' Mother said, studying my face, 'your story Bible and I'm sure Gertie would read it to her. Why don't you think on it, Matteus?'

I did think on it. And the more I thought on it, the more I knew that it would be a good thing to do. But I was also afraid that Gertie wouldn't take a Bible from me, even if it was a story Bible. She didn't, and had never, cared for Rev. Kruimel and still mentioned, from time to time, that the man had not remembered her name. So I devised a plan and asked Mother to wrap the book up carefully. She smiled at me, kissed me on my forehead, and said that she was proud of me. I was ten years old now and Liesl was almost five. She was a pretty child. Red-blondish curls danced on her shoulders and she had a dimple in her left cheek when she smiled. But she was shy of people and hid behind her mother's skirts if there was company. Yet she loved me and that was a thing that made me proud.

I had thought that the time to give Gertie the story Bible would be on Liesl's birthday. Mother thought that a good idea as well. On that day I took the package and put it in the carrier of my bicycle, as well as a top which I had carved with Father's help. It was a beautiful day and around me birds sang and crickets chirped. When I arrived at the house and knocked at the kitchen door, Liesl answered.

'Hello, M... M... Matteus,' she said with the distinct stutter that always showed up when she was excited or nervous.

'Happy birthday, Liesl,' I said, 'Here's a present for you.'

I gave her the top and she danced over to her mother with it, curls bouncing.

'M... M... Mother, look what M... M... Matteus gave me.'

Gertie smiled indulgently at her daughter.

'Did you tell him 'thank you', Liesl?'

'Oh no, I f... f... forgot.'

She ran back to me, gave me a kiss and said, 'thank you'. I walked into the kitchen and gave the package, wrapped in brown paper, to Gertie.

'What's this,' she asked.

'It's another present,' I said, 'It's not from me actually but from a man I met on the road. A peddler of some sort, I think. He said to give this to you for Liesl's birthday.'

Gertie took the package, brushing aside a strand of greying hair from her forehead. She felt the solidity of the package and knew it was not a dress or bonnet or some such gift.

'A peddler?' she questioned, as she sat down at the kitchen table gingerly beginning to unwrap the gift. 'And how did he happen to give you this for me?'

'Well,' I answered, looking past her at the blue cornflowers on the wallpaper, not finding it all that easy to lie, 'I don't really know who it was, but he seemed to know you and Liesl. He was sitting by the road against a hedge taking a rest. It almost seemed as if he were waiting for me. When I passed on my bike, he called out to me ...'

'Did he call you by name?' Gertie interrupted my fabrications.

'Yes,' I lied, 'he called out 'Matteus'.

Gertie had stopped unwrapping the package. Her eyes were intent on my face.

'Well,' she urged, as I had stopped talking, 'What then?'

'He asked if I was going to your farm and I said "Yes, I am." Then he took out the package from his backpack and handed it to me and said, "Please give this to Gerda."'

I purposely used Gerda's real name, not the Gertie it had evolved into after she had moved to Holland from Germany. She blanched at its use.

'Is that what he said?' she whispered, 'Gerda?'

'Yes,' I lied on quite cheerfully, quite certain now that she would accept the story Bible, 'and he also said that it was for you to read to Liesl.'

Gerda's hands finished their unwrapping. The story Bible lay on the table, unopened.

'It's a b... b... book for me,' Liesl's voice sang out, 'a real b... b... book, Mother.'

'Yes,' Gertie answered slowly, opening the book as if in a trance.

A sudden fear smote my heart. Oma had written my name on the first page. Had mother ripped that page out? It was impossible for me to find out without being obvious.

'Can you r... r... read it to me, Mother?'

'Yes, Liesl, I can but we'll save it for bedtime.'

'Are they stories, Mother? Oh, look, there are pictures too! C... c... can you read one now please, Mother?'

'No, not now. Before you go to bed. Why don't you go and play with the top that Matteus brought you?'

Liesl picked up the top, stole another glance at the Bible and ran outside. But a minute later, as I was getting ready to go to the barn, she came back in.

'Mother, who is the peddler?'

'Just someone who came to the door a long time ago, Liesl.'

'But why did he want to give me a p... p... present?'

'I don't know,' Gertie answered, 'I saw him once that long time ago, but I haven't seen him since.'

'When did you see him, Mother?'

'Before you were born.'

'Before I was born?'

'Yes,' Gertie said, her hand resting on her chin, 'and I do believe he was an angel.'

'What is an angel, Mother?'

'Someone sent by God, I suppose. Now go and play.'

Both Liesl and I went out. I to the barn and she to the cement patio to play with her top.

Time passed. Liesl began school when I was in grade five. At recess I said hello but it didn't do for boys to be seen fraternizing with little girls. I feared to be singled out and called "sissy". Even though I was still a good size for my age, there were boys who were taller and bigger than I was.

My father continued to work for Harmen Maritaans the occasional Saturday. It was a good, long walk though, and when he was offered part-time work by another farmer closer to the village, he gave Harmen notice. So I saw less and less of Gertie, Harmen and Liesl.

I was painfully aware that Liesl had very few friends at school and was sometimes teased mercilessly at recess. Firstly because she had reddish hair, secondly because her mother was German, and lastly because she still had that childish stutter which overwhelmed her whenever she was excited or nervous.

I distinctly recall a time when I was in grade eight that I was caught up in a group of children following Liesl as she walked home through a patch of forest to her country road. We were all shouting 'Liesl is a weasel!! Liesl is a weasel!!' She did not turn to face her tormentors, but simply walked on, back straight, head straight, red hair bobbing up and down, until we all grew tired of the game. I was glad she hadn't turned. Deep within myself I was horribly ashamed to have mocked her so. I recalled the times I had carried her about, had played games with her and had said that I would take care of her. It was also true that in spite of her stuttering, Liesl was easily the smartest girl at school in our one-room school house. Her marks were always very high and even at age nine, the schoolmaster would read her stories aloud to the rest of the class. He would read them because when she read out loud herself, her stutter always produced guffaws from other students even with the schoolmaster's threat of punishment.

I was hired on as a farmhand at a farm some ten miles from where we lived when I was fifteen. I loved farming and even though Mother encouraged me to continue schooling, Father said that a few years of hard work would put the delight of learning back into my heart. Only coming home on the weekends, I did not see much of anyone in the village.

And then it was war. Not that it changed matters that much for me in the beginning. Too young to join the army, I kept working. Liesl's mother died that first winter. There was a funeral in the church and people were reminded afresh that Gertie Maritaans had been a German.

Some of her relatives managed to come over from Germany for the funeral and they stayed on, much to the entire village's chagrin. There were three of them, two older women and a man, all in their fifties. The Maritaans, already not popular, were avoided even more and a rumour went about that they had Nazi leanings. If Liesl was teased before, now she was shunned and children would spit on her shadow. According to mother, she never retaliated.

On my days home, Mother would sometimes prod me and say, 'Oh, Matteus, shouldn't you visit Liesl sometimes? Remember how you used to play with her?'

'Why don't you go yourself?' I would answer and she would look at me with a strange, brooding look, almost as if she was about to tell me something. And then she would turn away.

I was seventeen when I joined the underground. It was exciting to be useful in the war effort, to deliver leaflets, to knock on doors to warn people that they should be going into hiding and to guide them to various farms in the neighbourhood past the Nazi posts that had been set up. It was almost easy for me, having been brought up in the area and knowing every twisting and turning out-of-the-way path in the district. In the beginning it was more of an adventure thing, I think, to do all these things. That is to say, it was an adventure until I saw the first Jews transported onto a train and sent on to a camp. Faces like Mother's face, faces like Father's face, and the children's faces – I can't begin to tell you about the children's faces. And the stories were that these were all being sent to their death; that they were being killed without mercy.

I could relate to you any number of stories. But there is only one, looking back now after all these years, that is with me most of the time, that is ingrained within my soul. And that is this story.

It was towards the end of the war. Our village had actually been fortunate in that it had lost very few men. It was the winter of 1944 and close to Christmas. The bitterly cold weather forced people to stay indoors. I was out on the road having just delivered some clandestine literature to an out-of-the-way farm. By chance I met Jan and Herman, also heading for and from my village, along the way. We were all looking forward to spending some time with our families. Snow crunched under our feet and we were in a jolly mood of sorts.

'Let's stop at the Maritaans' farm and see if the man has any potatoes left,' Jan Sikkens said.

We were close to the farm at the time.

'No, I've a better Idea,' Herman Tol replied, 'let's just sneak into his barn and take a look at whatever extra the man might have smuggled away.'

They clapped one another on the back and laughed. Fleetingly I remembered how kind Gertie and Harmen had been to my father and to myself and how I used to play with Liesl. But my emotions were numbed, even as my feet were numb with the cold. Oh, it was a cold, cold winter that winter of 1944. Jan began to tell a joke.

'Have you heard that every time the RAF bombs the German military targets in Holland, our newspapers are forced to report that no damage has been done but that "only a few cows have been killed"?'

He stopped and this time clapped me on the back.

'Pretty soon,' he continued with glee, 'Goebbels will have to unveil the statue of the 'Unknown Cow'.

I laughed along with Jan and Herman. After all, it was funny. Herman began another story as our feet turned into the lane-way leading to the Maritaans' farmhouse.

'Have you heard that a British barrage balloon,' he said, 'was drifting over a German aerodrome and that German fighters went up but totally missed the target? They tried again and again, but couldn't even come close to the mark.'

'What happened to the balloon?' Jan asked when Herman stopped short of finishing his story.

'It eventually burst from laughing,' Herman said and doubled over from laughter.

Except for the smoke curling up from its chimney, the Maritaans' farmhouse looked deserted. My mind became a book and its pages turned back to the time when I had been a small boy wearing bib overalls, carrying a hoe over my shoulder. My feet lagged – lagged and then stopped.

'Come on, Matteus,' Jan urged, 'the quicker we are, the less chance we have of being seen.'

'I don't think we should ...' I began, but Herman pulled me along mid-sentence.

'Come on,' he repeated Jan's words, 'Harmen is a Nazi sympathizer. Don't wind up on a guilt trip. He's bound to have some contraband stuff in the barn. If we don't take it the Nazis will. I don't know about your mother, but mine will jump for joy if I bring her something good to eat for Christmas.'

We had reached the milk-house and Jan opened the door and walked in. Behind the cooler I could see a small child on the floor playing with a kitten. The child was sturdy, well-fed and content. The child was me and under the cooler I could see Gertie's black stockings as she scoured the cooler. But Gertie was dead.

'Come on, Matteus.'

I followed Jan and Herman into the barn. What would I say to Harmen if he was there? In the semi-darkness I could see several cows in their stalls and I smelled a mixture of old hay and manure. And again I saw the child I had been walking down the rows, a child who received a nod of approval every now and then from Harmen for doing his best.

'I bet he has some food stored in the loft,' Herman said in a loud whisper as we edged our way over to the ladder.

'W... W... What are you doing here?'

It was Liesl. She emerged from the shadows and stood in front of us carrying a pail of milk and wearing a shawl. At first no one said anything. A flush crept over my cheeks and I started to speak when a noise in the yard alerted us. There were voices – loud, rough, German voices. Liesl, without meaning to, I think, grabbed my arm.

'They have come,' she whispered and then, 'I knew they w... w... would sooner or later. I knew it.'

'Who?' I asked, 'are they?'

'The Nazis,' she answered.

Herman and Jan motioned that we should hide. We climbed up the ladder. Jan first, Herman second, Liesl third and myself last. Up in the loft we crawled towards the side wall facing the yard and through the cracks in the barn beams could see that Liesl had been right. The Gestapo stood in the yard. I counted a contingent of some eight men who were surrounding the house, even as one approached the kitchen door.

'Öffnen – Open,' he shouted, but the door stayed shut.

The smoke from the chimney still curled up, neatly, as if nothing was wrong. Next to me, Liesl was rigid and I patted her arm.

'Öffnen.'

The officer shouted again, simultaneously kicking the door with his boot. It flew open and light flooded out from the warmth of the kitchen. Harmen appeared in the opening.

'Heraus! Alles heraus! Los! – Out. All out. Quickly!'

'Oh, Father!'

I heard Liesl whisper next to me and the sound was so heart wrenching that I put my arm about her.

Harmen did not stand in the door opening long. He was shoved inside, not outside as the officer had ordered. The officer as well, followed by two of his men, disappeared inside. Without rhyme or reason I thought of the caption Jan had jokingly referred to half an hour ago – 'Statue to an unknown cow'. What had Harmen done to anger his Nazi friends. Jan put my thoughts into words.

'Did your father cheat on his friends, Liesl?'

Liesl sobbed but did not answer, her eyes riveted on the house as she peered through the cracks. The door had closed behind the Germans and we could hear nothing for a few moments. But then it opened again and Harmen was pushed out. The officer followed him and behind him three other people emerged. Liesl stiffened even more. I patted her shoulder awkwardly. It must be tough, I thought to myself, to see your family, even though they were traitors, mishandled.

'Marchieren! Los! Los! March! Quickly! Quickly!'

'Will they come looking for Liesl too?' Herman asked.

'I don't know,' I answered, 'but we can't ...'

I didn't finish my sentence because it wasn't necessary to surmise if they would come for her or not. From all appearances the entire group was marching down the lane and away from the farm. We watched as they slowly disappeared.

'What did your father do, Liesl?'

I softly spoke directly into her ear. She shook off my arm and stood up. Her shawl fell into the hay. Her red hair, half-hidden under a kerchief curled onto her forehead and her cheeks.

'D... D... Do?' she repeated, loud enough for Jan and Herman to hear, and again, 'D... D... Do?'

'Y... Y... Yes,' Herman mocked, 'W... W... What has he d... d... done?'

'He m... m... married a Jew,' she answered. 'He m... m... married my m... m... m... other and those people are m.. m.. my aunts and uncle. They were living with us.'

We were shocked into silence, all three of us. Jan even had to grace to blush.

'I'm sorry, Liesl,' he said, 'I'm so sorry. I'm a big oaf.'

Herman as well offered Liesl his apologies. But no words came out of my mouth and I discovered that I was weeping.

'We'll follow,' Jan said, 'at a distance, of course. But I know that we can get some of the other men together and we'll think of a plan.

'I'm c... c... coming too,' Liesl said and was the first down the ladder.

She ran through the barn, to the milk-house and, I presume, out the door. I was behind her, but tripped over the milk pail standing at the foot of the ladder. The milk ran into the gutter, white onto black, pure onto stink. We made our way through the barn as well, and walked through the milk-house, waiting outside for Liesl who had gone into the house. She joined us a moment later, wearing a heavy blue coat and white mittens. I recognized the coat. It had been Gertie's.

'Well,' Herman said, beginning to walk towards the lane, 'better get started.'

Herman and Jan walked in front and I walked behind them with Liesl. We passed the yard, the place where the vegetable garden had been, the place where Rev. Kruimel had fallen down and the place where I had said the peddler had given me the story Bible. The blue coat trudged along next to me. I was not focused so much on how to free Liesl's relatives as I was concentrating on what to say to Liesl, to explain to her that I was so ashamed. Jan was naming all the young men we could count on and Herman was nodding vigorously. Every few minutes one of them would smile at Liesl to demonstrate their zeal in helping. Liesl was quiet, but after fifteen minutes of steady walking she turned to me with a small smile.

'Thank you, Matteus.'

'For what?' I answered.

'For your gift,' she answered.

'Gift?'

'Yes, remember my b.. b.. birthday gift? The one you said the peddler b... b... brought?'

I nodded. I did surely remember.

'I knew it was not from a peddler,' she went on, 'b.. b.. but from you. M... M... Mother knew it too, b... b... but she didn't mind.'

She was quiet again for a long time and so was I and then she whispered again.

'M... M... Mother read it to me and Father every d... d... day after supper.'

'She did?'

'Yes. She never m... m... missed.'

'I'm glad,' I answered, and I was glad.

I took a quick glance at Liesl's face and swore within myself that I would never again let peer pressure or fear dictate what I would say or do. The village lay ahead of us. The church spire glinted in the rather harsh light of the sinking sun.

'I rather think,' Jan turned as he spoke, 'that they would put any prisoners into the old schoolhouse. Last I heard, the soldiers were quartered at the train station and there are no other large buildings except for the church. What do you think?'

I shrugged but Herman responded that he also thought this was a good possibility but that we should first get some of the other men together before checking it out.

Then he added, 'Where should we bring Harmen and his relatives if an escape plan succeeds?'

'Willem will know,' I said, 'there are a few hiding places in the woods and God is with us in that it is snowing. There will be no tracks.'

Willem Proost was the head of the underground movement in our district. They both nodded and grinned. The truth of it was that both Jan and Herman thrived on danger and enjoyed these escapades.

'And what about Liesl?' Jan asked, 'Where will she go?'

'To my house,' I answered curtly, 'Liesl is going to my house. My mother will ...'

'But first,' Liesl interrupted, 'first I will come with you.'

And nothing we said could dissuade her.

We were in the village now and went to Willem's home. That is to say, we first separated. Jan went one way and

Herman another. But I took Liesl directly to Willem's house. Fifteen minutes later Jan showed up and some fifteen minutes after that, Herman arrived. Three other men came as well. They all eyed Liesl suspiciously but they all knew Harmen had been arrested together with his house guests. To my surprise, they did not all believe Liesl's story, discounting the fact that her mother had been Jewish and that the people now in German custody were relatives. Some remained convinced that the whole 'Maritaans' lot', as they phrased it, were German collaborators and had now been caught cheating on their benefactors in some unsavoury business deal. In fact, two of the men were so adamant that this was the case, that they left, having 'better' things to do on Christmas Eve.

'They are being held,' Willem said after some discussion, 'in the school, just as you thought. Three soldiers are standing guard and that's the problem. They are heavily armed. The school door is not hard to open, but how can we ...'

'I... I... I know,' Liesl said.

We all stared at her. She had sat so quietly in a corner of the room we had all but forgotten she was there.

'I... I...,' Liesl began again, rather helplessly.

She hated her stutter, I know. There was an embarrassed silence and then the men began to speak again, suggesting different tactics and diversions. But Liesl stood up.

'G... G... Get Rev. Kruimel to open the church next d... d... door to the school,' she said, 'and tell him to turn on the l... l... lights. I will ask the m... m... men to come to the church.'

'But why would they leave the school and come to the church, child?' Willem asked.

Liesl straightened her shoulders and I saw her walking straight ahead of the group of children who had taunted her. And I had been one of them.

'B... B... Because they will,' Liesl answered Willem, 'I... I... I know they will. And then you can let my f... f... father and my aunts and uncle out.'

It was quiet. We all looked at one another.

'If I c... c... can't do it,' Liesl added, 'then you can try something else. P... P... Please let me try.'

Willem nodded. 'I think,' he said to us, 'that there is not a great danger that the soldiers on guard will know that she is Harmen's daughter. Very well, child,' he went on, turning to Liesl, 'Are you sure?'

She nodded.

'Well, then we'll try it.'

He scraped his chair back from the table and stood up.

'Jan, go to Rev. Kruimel and explain the situation to him. Ask him to do as Liesl said. It should take you only about ten minutes. We'll wait fifteen and then Liesl will walk over to the school house. We'll follow at a distance a minute or two later and then we'll see what happens.'

Jan left. Willem sat down again and we waited. Willem's wife had poured us some surrogate[11] coffee. I drank mine but Liesl didn't touch a drop of hers. She stared at the carpet and had her hands clasped together in her lap. When Willem stood up again to say that it was time to go, Liesl turned her face to me. She smiled and despite the fact that she was fast on her way to becoming a young and beautiful woman, she looked so much like the child I had known that I swallowed.

'Thank you again, M... M... Matteus,' she said.

Then she put on her blue coat, walked towards the door, opened it and disappeared into the street.

'I am the Door.' My thoughts jumbled and I could see the words in the big Bible mother had given me on my twelfth birthday. Willem coughed

'I should have prayed with her,' he said, 'but let's pray for her now.'

We all took off our hats and Willem prayed.

'Please take care of Liesl, Father. Keep her in your care and let this evening have a joyous ending to Your glory. Amen.'

We made our way in pairs, over to the church and the school, each approaching the area from a different direction. I arrived just in time to see Liesl approach the soldier who was stationed outside the school building.

'G... G... Gutenabend - Good evening.'

The soldier was not averse to greeting a pretty girl and he did so.

'M... m... morgen ist Weihnachts und,' Liesl faltered, 'und ich will dich einladen ... nur nach dir Kirche zu k... k... kommen. Tomorrow is Christmas, and I want to invite you to come to church now.'

Her stuttering was increasing and I began to sweat. No soldiers would leave their posts at the invitation of a young girl to come to church. But although she stuttered, Liesl's German was impeccable. Gertie had taught her well.

'Ich s... s... soll für ihm s... s... singen. I shall sing for you,' she went on.

The soldier laughed. He opened the school door and beckoned to the other two soldiers.

'Ein mädchen soll für uns singen – a girl will sing for us,' he said, 'aber sie stotters – but she stutters.'

He laughed again and they joined him. The picture of the blue coat blurred in my eyes that were now filled both with anger and tears. But I was no better than those soldiers. Had not I, Matteus VanderSloot mocked Liesl as she was going home. 'Liesl is a weasel ...' I heard the words resound in my mind, until another sound encompassed it.

Stille Nacht, heilige Nacht!

Alles schläft, einsam wacht

Nur das traute, hochheilige Paar.

Holder Knabe im luckigen Haar,

Schlaf in himmlischer Ruh,

Schlaf in himmlischer Ruh.

Liesl was singing. Her 'Silent Night' intertwined with the snowflakes. Her voice, pure and clear, filled the street. The only light was the light from the stars and from the open school door. Vaguely in the background I could see Harmen and the others sitting on the floor of the classroom.

The soldiers stood in the doorway, silently surveying the girl whose head was being covered with a small, soft hood of snow. Her face lifted up, she sang on and the second stanza was even a sweeter rendition than the first. I had not known that she could sing like this and there was not even a hint of the stuttering that so plagued her when she spoke to others.

Stille Nacht, heilige Nacht!

Hirten erst kund gemacht;

Durch der Engel Halleluja

Tönt es laut von fern and nah:

Christ, der Retter, is da.

Christ, der Retter, is da.

Liesl's voice rang on. There was no hesitation, no stop, and the soldiers stood next to one another, quiet and subdued. After she had finished the third stanza, one of them wiped his eyes on his sleeve and put down his gun. Liesl, still singing, turned and began walking towards the church which was now flooded with light.

Er ist ein Ros' entsprungen

Aus einer Wurzel zart,

Wie unse die Alten sungen,

Von Jesse kam die Art,

Und hat ein blümlein bracht,

Mitten im kalten Winter

Wohl zu der halben Nacht.

Gertie had taught Liesl. I could see Gertie now but her figure faded into the figure of Liesl, ever singing and ever walking towards the open door of the church. I held my breath. The snow wreathed Liesl's hair and she looked for all the world as to what I imagined an angel to look like. Gertie had thought that the peddler was an angel. Maybe he had been. I followed Liesl's steps with amazement until a loud bang made me jump. One of the soldiers had slammed the door to the school house shut and, taking a few steps away from the door, beckoned his two comrades to follow him to the church.

'Es ist Weihnachts' abend – It is Christmas Eve,' he said, and his words carried through the incredibly pure sound of the singing, 'und die gefangenen können nicht weglaufen – and the prisoners cannot run away.'

The two looked at one another and shrugged.

'Warum nicht? – Why not?'

And they followed Liesl's tracks, making their way over and into the church.

Das Blümelein so kleine,

Das duftet uns so süss;

Mit seinem hellen Scheine

Vertreibt's die Finsternis.

Wahr' Mensch und wahrer Gott,

Hilft uns aus allen Leiden,

Rettet von Sünd und Tod.

It was only a small trick for us to force the lock and get Harmen and the others away while Liesl continued her singing for the soldiers in the church. What we had not thought about was how to get Liesl away afterwards. She was shot and died in the snow in front of the church a few hours later.

Willem had prayed that the evening might have a joyous ending. I could not see it at the time, but later, much later understood that the Birth can never be separated from the gift of the Death. And Liesl had received that gift – had received it with an open heart.

'Better is the end of a thing than its beginning,
and the patient in spirit is better
than the proud in spirit.'
Ecclesiastes 7:8

THE END OF A THING

O ur village in northern Holland had never been very large, but those first few years following the second world war, it seemed especially small. A number of men had died at the hands of the Germans; others had died of starvation that last hunger winter of 1944; and still others had moved away to cities and to jobs. With the exception of a large hospital just on the outskirts of the village, a hospital which served the whole district, there was nothing unusual about our village. As many other villages, it was a little world within the world. Everyone knew who everyone else was, what they were doing and what they were going to do. And why shouldn't they? Most of them belonged to the same church, except for the few Roman Catholic families scattered here and there. Children attended the same school; parents went to the same grocery store; and the baker baked the same bread for all of them. When it rained or when it did not rain, when someone was ill, got married or died, or when a child left to attend university in the big city, it was a community affair.

It was a long time ago, but a tiny incident stands out in my memory. Walking down the main street one day when I was about twelve or thirteen years old, part of a larger group of girls, all of us stopped suddenly because one of the girls noticed that the 'for sale' sign in front of the Lander house was gone. Bert Lander was a retired farmer who had built a monstrosity of a house in the middle of the village back in the 30s. He had not had the pleasure of living in it for a very long time, because he had died of a massive stroke only a year after he moved into it. His wife had not long outlived him.

The children, none of whom had become farmers and none of whom wanted to live in our village, had rented the house to various people, most of whom had been lawyers, doctors and other studied people. But for some reason, the house was never occupied for a very long period. At any rate, it had recently been put up for sale, and now the sign was gone. Unashamedly, we walked up to the windows and peeked in. There was no sign of life. Whoever was to move in had not arrived.

A few days later a moving van stood in front of the house. Again we traipsed over and watched as furniture was unloaded. A black shining baby grand piano brought sighs, and a couch meant to drown owners in its puffy opulence, left us breathless. And so it went on. Whoever it was who had bought the place, was wealthy, extremely wealthy. There was no doubt about it. But when we tried to satisfy our curiosity by once more peeping through the windows the next day, the curtains had been drawn and we were left unsatisfied.

The following week, however, a new girl stepped into our classroom. She did not knock, but opened the door as if she was the headmaster. Walking straight, head held high, she did not seem the least bit intimidated by the fact that she was facing a room full of inquisitive children. For I have to admit that we all stared most unashamedly. She made her way to front and stopped short next to our teacher. He rather took it in stride.

'You must be Sanna Klok,' he said calmly.

There was not much that upset Mr. Kits. He was in his fifties, balding and ate tiny little diamond liquorice out of a small blue box underneath his lectern throughout the day. We thought it was because his wife did not let him have any sort of candy at home. She was a very thin, anorexic-looking woman and it was said that she hid food in the attic for fear of the Germans coming back.

'Class, please welcome Sanna,' Mr. Kits continued.

'Welcome, Sanna,' we repeated rather parrot-like, never taking our eyes off Sanna and her blue velvet dress – a dress with pleats and a white lace collar.

The room was arranged two to a seat. Mr. Kits pointed to the only available empty seat in the class – the one next to myself. Sanna made her way through the middle aisle. I sat in the last row. Initially my place had been in the front row but that had changed when Marcus Rook had been diagnosed with myopic vision, something which had sounded very romantic but which simply meant he was near-sighted. Sanna, everyone noted as she walked towards the back of the classroom, had a small straight nose, dark blue eyes with very long black lashes, a pale complexion, and blond, shoulder-length hair that curled at the edges. The boys gaped and so did the girls, truth be known. Before she sat down, Sanna took a long, hard look at me. I suppose I passed muster, because she permitted herself a small, stiff smile. I smiled back trying to appear indifferent to the fact that everyone was turning around looking at us, and helped her find her place in the various subjects we were taught that morning.

At recess, all the girls crowded around Sanna. But she gave away very little, safe for the fact that her father was a business man, that her mother had died when she was born and that she had no brothers or sisters. It rapidly became apparent that first week, that Sanna was a wizard in most subjects. She spoke fluent English, French, and German, and literally danced her way through the rigours of Algebra.

'Tutors', she explained her incredible talent away, 'I've always had tutors. My father wants me to do well.'

No one at school had ever had tutors. The girls in class eyed Sanna with a new kind of awe, which had begun when they noted with a certain amount of incredulity that her fingernails were polished and that she applied an almost unnoticeable amount of lipstick to her two small round lips. I sometimes bit mine to make them red, but I had begun to hide my short fingernails under books whenever the difference between our hands became too obvious.

In the month that followed, Sanna made almost exclusive friends with Anne, the daughter of the greengrocer. Anne was a lamb, a follower. That is to say, she slavishly swallowed any attention given to her and generally speaking, always did what someone else told her to do. A nondescript girl with brownish hair and a few freckles on her cheeks, she wore clothes that had been handed down to her by three older sisters. Why Sanna had chosen her of all the girls in class to chum around with, was a source of wonder. But she seemed to love going to the grocer's house. She had to be told at times, Anne's mother told my mother, to leave.

Sanna also marked me, every now and then, with her graces, especially on Sunday. She would often come to our pew, smile at Mother and sit down next to us. Perhaps because Father was the minister and because she felt there was some spiritual significance to hobnobbing with me on that day, she sought me out. Her father rarely came along to church. He was often out of town on business. Mother who encouraged me in the friendship, pointed out frequently that Sanna, after all, did not have a mother and had to contend with a housekeeper to teach her manners and to give her affection. She often said this when she tucked me in at night and I spilled out some grievance that I had been harbouring most of the day.

There was a middle-aged woman in town, a Mrs. Smit, the local seamstress, whom Sanna, for some inexplicable reason, disliked. Whenever she saw Mrs. Smit walk across the street, and the woman had a slight limp, she would mimic her. I never once saw her come close to the woman, never saw her engage her in speech. But from a distance she would make fun of her and I don't know how Anne could stomach the mocking. Perhaps she was just too naive. Mrs. Smit was a gentle woman. I liked her. She had made me a green dress the previous summer, taking the time to measure carefully and to compliment me on the fact that I was growing taller. Yes, I liked her. No one in the village was exactly sure where she hailed from and it had been the subject of many lively discussions. She had only lived in the district for some three years. Long enough, though, to win the respect of a great many mothers whom she helped with this and that.

'Dorcas,' my mother said, 'her name should have been Dorcas Smit.'

It was close to Easter and Mr. Kits had told us the Bible story about Thomas, disbelieving Thomas. For being a quiet man, Mr. Kits was an avid and very descriptive storyteller. It was almost as if he came alive during that time each morning when he explained and retold Scripture stories in his own words. His eyes glowed and his hands moved about as he searched for and found just the right words to emphasize a point. He usually had the entire class in the palm of his hand.

We had all been struck with the horrible dismay and mortal fear Cain had felt after God spoke to him of his misdeed; we had all sweated along with Noah in the construction of the ark, a much more difficult building to construct than farmer Blom's newly erected silo; and we were all convinced that Abraham had probably looked somewhat like Mr. Korman, whose long beard was a source of curiosity.

It was very quiet in the class as Mr. Kits spoke.

'Thomas was not there the first time that Jesus appeared to the other disciples. But he was one of the twelve. He should have been there.'

Mr. Kits looked at us over the thin gold rim of his glasses as if we were all Thomases and as if we had all somehow missed the opportunity that Thomas had thrown away.

'Consequently, Thomas did not have peace. He was miserable and downcast. He had no rest within himself. And this was even though the other disciples kept telling him 'We have seen the Lord, Thomas. We know He lives.'

Next to me, Sanna fidgeted. She was uncomfortable. I could sense it. Staring out the window, I wondered if she heard anything that Mr. Kits was saying.

'If we miss something that God puts on our way, and other people tell us about it, we should never be so stubborn as to not listen.'

Sanna sighed. It was a big sigh and went straight down the centre aisle, through the window and onto the street. Everyone heard it and heads twisted around. Mr. Kits stopped his discourse.

'Miss Klok, perhaps you would be kind enough to tell the class what has been said these last five minutes?'

Sanna's head turned. She looked at Mr. Kits, but there was a faraway look in her eyes. I knew she didn't really see him.

'What you said?' she repeated dully, 'Yes, I can tell you that. You were talking about Thomas, doubting Thomas. He did not believe that Jesus had really come back. And he should have believed.'

It was very quiet in class. Sanna spoke in a monotone, as if she were reciting a lesson. She went on.

'But I don't blame him for not believing. I think that Jesus should have showed him in some other way that He was still alive. Maybe Thomas missed out because he was locked up somewhere and couldn't get out. Maybe he just couldn't make the meeting with the other disciples through no fault of his own. I think you should put that into your story as well. That's what I think.'

There was no sound for a bit. Everyone digested what Sanna had said. Mr. Kits tapped his fingers on his lectern.

'I'm happy to know that you were, after all, listening, Miss Klok,' he finally said, and then he continued with the story as if there had been no interruption.

That day, Sanna ran away across the playground after school and even Anne, the greengrocer's daughter, was left to walk home alone.

That following Sunday, putting her arm through mine after we had shuffled down the aisle at the end of the service, Sanna pulled Anne and myself into the bathroom behind her. It was a small bathroom, only boasting a tiny sink and one small toilet cubicle.

'I thought the sermon would never end,' she sighed, as she pushed a thick blond lock over her right shoulder and eyed herself in the mirror.

There was a noise in one of the cubicles, warning us there was someone else present, but Sanna paid no heed. I flushed at the comment. Not that I listened to sermons as attentively as I should, but it was my father, after all, who preached them. Anne giggled softly, simultaneously making big eyes at me rather apprehensively. Squashed against the wall, she waited patiently to be told when it was time to leave.

'Did you see Mrs. Smit's coat?'

Sanna's voice was derisive. She pulled the old blue towel off the towel rack, draped it around her shoulders and pranced around. Not that you could actually prance around in the small space permitted but she did seem to manage it.

'How anyone can wear something so outdated and moth-eaten is amazing! Don't you think so, Anne?'

Anne nodded half-heartedly.

'And then,' Sanna continued, 'the woman sits in one of the front pews where everyone is forced to look at that awful, awful coat.'

'Well,' I interrupted, running the tap and beginning to wash my hands as I spoke, 'she is a little hard of hearing and being close to the front helps. Besides that, I rather like her coat.'

The noise of the tap-water hitting the sink, cushioned my words somewhat.

'That's silly, Nelly,' Sanna bit back at me, 'And what do you know about fashions anyway? The truth is, Mrs. Smit's coat dates from the year zero and she smells like mothballs.'

'Well,' Anne said, biting her nails and then looking up, 'I think I have to go. We're getting company for lunch and Ma said I should be home shortly after the service.

She moved towards the door and if my hands had not been wet, I would have been right out the door with her. But as it was, I grabbed the towel off Sanna's back just as Anne threw a "goodbye" over her shoulder. Sanna grinned at me, and followed Anne out the door.

'Maybe I can go there for lunch,' she sang out before the door shut.

The toilet flushed in the cubicle and to my horror, Mrs. Smit walked out.

'Hello, Nelly,' she calmly said, as she moved towards the sink.

I dried my hands and hung the towel back up on the rack.

'Hello, Mrs. Smit,' I responded and then, without another word, I also walked out.

When I came home from school on Monday, Mother told me that the Kloks would be joining us for supper that evening.

'Why?'

I threw the word out rather angrily and Mother looked at me as if I were a stranger. She didn't know about the Smit fiasco. I had planned to avoid Sanna all day, but she was not at school.

'Go and do your homework, Nelly,' was all the reply I got.

When the supper bell rang, I slow-footed it down the stairs and into the dining-room. Mr. Klok and Father were already seated and Mother called me into the kitchen to carry in the salad.

'I didn't see Sanna,' I said as I picked up the yellow salad bowl.

'She wasn't feeling well today and is staying home with Mrs. Appel.

Mrs. Appel was the housekeeper and a very jolly lady she was too. Round like a dumpling, you disappeared into her bosom when she hugged you.

'Oh,' I replied and felt a trifle more comfortable about the next hour.

Supper went well. Mr. Klok was a nice man. Sometimes I wondered why, because she was surrounded by such admirable people, Sanna had turned out to be such a domineering child. We had brussels sprouts that evening. Not my favourite and Mr. Klok, who sat next to me and saw me poking at the green little cabbage mounds on my plate, took several onto his own while Mother was not looking. I suspect Father saw, but he didn't say anything. After Bible reading and prayer, as Mother got up to clear the table and as I also pushed back my chair to get up and help, Mr. Klok asked her to sit down again.

'I can't stay long,' he said, 'but I just wanted to say ... I wanted you all to know that I do so appreciate the friendship that you have shown, both to me and to Sanna.'

Father began to reply, but Mr. Klok waved his hand to indicate that he was not done speaking. 'I want to tell you,' he said in his rather deep voice, 'why I came here. To this village, I mean, and why I didn't settle in some other part of Holland.'

Mother sat down again and I stayed where I was, chair pushed out, a trifle behind Mr. Klok.

'You didn't know, my wife,' Mr. Klok went on, 'When I use the past tense it sounds as if she is ... well, as if she has died. And I don't know whether or not that is the case.'

'But,' I interrupted quite rudely, 'Sanna said ...'

A look from both Mother and Father stopped me. Mr. Klok paid no attention to the interruption. He ran his hand through his thinning, reddish hair and then put his elbows on the table, resting his cheeks on his hands. He had long hands, an artist's hands and his nails were quite a bit cleaner than mine. I remembered Sanna's manicured, polished nails and inadvertently glanced down.

'I met my wife in the late 1920s.' Mr. Klok was now speaking to the wall opposite the table. 'She worked in one of the stores which I regularly had to deal with on my travels. She was a couturière and was very good at what she was doing.'

'Couturière?' I repeated slowly, earning me more stern looks from my parents.

But Mr. Klok turned around and smiled at me.

'It's a hard word, isn't it, Nelly? It means someone who designs, makes and sells clothes, fashionable clothes.'

'Oh,' I said and repeated the word in my mind several times over. It sounded sophisticated and lovely.

'We fell in love and were married.' Mr. Klok put his elbows back on the table and continued his story. 'It was not too difficult at that time yet to marry a Jew.'

'She was Jewish?'

This time Father interrupted.

'Yes, she was. My wife was a Jew. But not a practicing Jew. She converted to Christianity when she was a child. Her parents, who both died while she was a teenager, were members of the Lutheran church.'

'Hmm,' was all my father permitted himself to say.

'We had no children. That is to say, Sarah was very delicate. Her health was not good. After we had been married about three years, she was diagnosed with tuberculosis.'

Mother clucked. I wasn't sure exactly what tuberculosis was, but I had seen the little tents in the village. Tom Vlietman had been in one for about a year and then he had died. So had Leny Olster.

'I sent her to a sanatorium. Our doctor recommended a very good one in Switzerland. It cost a lot of money but I was able to manage. I visited her regularly. It was a hard time, a hard time for both of us. Then just prior to Christmas 1934, the doctor told me that humanly speaking there was very little hope – that Sarah could not possibly live another year. 'She wants to come home for the holidays,' he said, 'and I don't see why she can't spend a few days of what will likely be her last months, in her home surroundings."

Mother's eyes were riveted on Mr. Klok's face. I knew she was close to tears. Mother always empathized wholeheartedly with everyone. That's why all the people I was acquainted with, including the milkman, were always ready to tell her whatever his or her troubles were. I knew, because I'd certainly told her mine many times.

'It was a wonderful Christmas. It was so special ...'

Mr. Klok's voice broke but then he continued.

'After a few weeks back at the sanatorium, it came to light that Sarah was pregnant. She was expecting our first child.'

Mother smiled. It was a slow smile. I wondered what Sanna thought of this story.

'Everyone at the sanatorium was furious with me. 'Poor Sarah,' they said, 'one foot in the grave and now she is pregnant as well'. They wanted her to give them permission to abort the baby but Sarah, my sweet, defenceless wife, became a lioness. She would hold her hands over her belly and rock as if she was already holding a little one. There was no arguing with her. She would keep the child and that was that.'

'Good for her,' Father said and Mother nodded.

'And the strange thing was,' Mr. Klok went on, sitting up straight and pounding the table as he spoke, 'the strange thing was, that what the doctors and nurses had not been able to accomplish by any sort of nursing or medicine or diet, that God-given pregnancy accomplished. The growth of tiny Sanna in her belly, pushed up her rib cage and healed her.'

Mother's smile grew broader and I grinned.

'That amazing,' she said.

'God was good to us,' Mr. Klok continued, 'but then things became very difficult in Germany, as I'm sure you know.'

'Yes,' Father said, 'but how is it that a Dutchman like yourself, was situated in Germany?'

'Well, I wasn't really,' Mr. Klok replied, 'it's just that some of the companies I dealt with were located there. Then, because Sarah had been born in Germany and had a nice apartment, we decided to stay there after we were married. I still travelled to different places, but Sarah was much taken up with the child. They had a very special relationship, the two of them.'

He sighed and continued. 'For a number of years I was able to continue in my business. We had obtained identity cards for

Sarah and Sanna – Aryan identity cards. But somehow, and I don't know how, someone pointed a finger at Sarah. One day I came home from a business trip to find her gone. The Gestapo had taken her away.' He stopped and wiped his hands on his pants. There was sweat on his forehead. I could see it glisten under the lamp. He blinked nervously and Mother offered him some water.

'No, thanks. Please forgive me. Always, always when I come to this part in my thoughts, I think that perhaps I should have done something else – that I should have moved back to Holland sooner. That maybe if I had acted differently, she might have been kept from suffering.'

'Did you find out where she was – where the Gestapo had taken her?'

The question popped out of my mouth before I realized it. 'Little girls should be seen and not heard.' I could hear the unspoken phrase loud and clear. Didn't I know it? I looked down at my lap to avoid Father's gaze. Mr. Klok turned around to look at me.

'No, I could not find out, Nelly. It was as if she had never been. But little Sanna ... I found little Sanna in a hiding place we had fashioned together behind a partition in the bedroom wall. The child was terrified, and would not speak for a long time.'

'Then why does Sanna tell everyone that her mother died when she was born?'

'For a while she was afraid to tell people that she was half-Jewish. She saw so many people beaten up and taken away never to be heard from again.'

'What happened after you came back home – after Sarah, your wife, had disappeared, I mean?'

This time it was Mother who spoke.

'Well, as I said before, I exhausted my resources in trying to find out where Sarah had been taken, but I met with walls everywhere. Either people were afraid to speak or they would not. After a few months I took the child, I took Sanna, and left Germany. It was still possible and I had to get her, in any case, to a safe haven. Then, after the war, when people began to trickle back from concentration camps, I heard rumours that Sarah might have survived – that some people thought they might have seen her.'

'And had they?'

Mr. Klok turned again and smiled at me.

'I think they had and the Red Cross said that possibly a woman who fit the description of my wife, Sarah, had travelled to England and from there seemed to have gone on to Holland, to the northern provinces.'

'Does Sanna know that you are looking for her?' Mother asked.

'Well, yes and no. Yes, she knows that perhaps her mother is still alive and also that I make it my business to search out people who might have some tiny bit of information regarding her whereabouts. And no, she does not seem to be interested. She does not want to speak of her mother or of the time past.'

'Was she ever mistreated?'

'No, not really. That is to say, she, of course, spent many hours alone and has not really had for many years the benefit of a mother's love, a mother's care.'

I almost felt sorry for Sanna, until I remembered how unkind she had been to Mrs. Smit. There was no excuse, was there?

'She, my Sarah, had a small birthmark on her left wrist. Actually it was a bit higher than her wrist. She used to say that if I would see only her arm, I would always know her.'

Mr. Klok pushed his chair back abruptly.

'Well, I just wanted you to know. I'm aware that people are saying that Sanna has not got a mother, and this might be true. But I must, you understand, I must continue in my search for Sarah. It was perhaps my fault that she was taken. I should have moved out of Germany sooner, but I never thought ... I just never thought ...'

He stood up and the serviette which had lain in his lap, fell to the floor. I bent over to pick it up and he patted my head.

'You are a good girl, Nelly. Thank you for being friends with Sanna.'

I flushed and put the serviette on the table.

'That's all right, Mr. Klok.'

A week later, Father called me into his study.

'Close the door behind you, Nelly,' he said, as he sat behind the typewriter on his desk.

I closed the door a little apprehensively. Father sounded very serious.

'I spoke with Mrs. Boon this morning.'

Mrs. Boon was the greengrocer's wife and Anne's mother. I felt myself growing more apprehensive.

'It seems that Mrs. Boon heard from Anne that some girls made fun of Mrs. Smit last Sunday. Is that so, Nelly?'

I looked down. I had thought, because nothing had happened, that the incident would pass without notice. That is to say, I had hoped that it would. I had not expected Anne to talk to her mother, but had rather wished that she would talk to Sanna and convince her to apologize for her rude words.

'Well, Nelly?'

'Yes, it's true.'

'Do you want to tell me about it?'

I began to fidget with my hands. I'd rather not tell Father about it actually. What his question really meant was, 'You have to tell me about it.' So there I was.

'Sit down, Nelly.'

I walked towards the desk and sat opposite Father. He took a puff of his pipe, put it in the ashtray and folded his arms.

'Before you tell me,' Father said, 'I want you to know that yesterday Mrs. Smit had a small heart attack. She's in the hospital. I think she will be all right, but ...'

'I'm sorry.'

I looked up and met Father's intent gaze head on.

'I am sorry, Father. Honest.'

'Well, why don't you tell me exactly what happened.'

The upshot of the whole matter was that Father went to speak to Mr. Klok and that Mr. Klok, Sanna and myself were on our way to the hospital within the hour.

My shoes made a lot of noise on the tiles of the hospital corridor. Sanna's shoes must have had rubber soles, because she made no noise at all. She walked on the other side of her father, and he held her hand. I had mine stuffed into the pockets of my coat.

'Why do I have to go too? I wasn't rude to Mrs. Smit.'

'Because you didn't speak up enough, Nelly. And that is a sin of omission. What if someone had said something nasty about Mother, or about me?'

I flushed, remembering what Sanna had said about the sermon.

'All right, I'll go.'

The corridor was long and the place smelled as if no one ever made hachee, fried onions mixed with potatoes and vegetables. It was my favourite dish and no one made it like Mother.

'Yes, how can I help you?'

We were at the desk, and Mr. Klok let go of Sanna's hand.

'We are here to visit Mrs. Smit.'

'Mrs. Smit? Umh, yes, room 244. Up the stairs on your right. But children ...'

'I'm fourteen,' Sanna divulged with a certain amount of pride.

Looking at her as she stood defiantly in front of the desk on her rubber soles, I did not see how the nurse could refuse her. But neither did I not understand why Sanna would want to be allowed to go to visit Mrs. Smit. After all, she had antagonized the woman.

'Well,' the nurse hesitated.

'Both these girls are good friends of Mrs. Smit. It will do her so much good to see them,' Mr. Klok intervened. 'And I understand she has no other relatives. So please let them go up.'

'Well, all right. But you must promise not to stay long.'

We walked up the stairs one at a time. It was a thin stairs, one which could not bear the pairing of people. Sanna was first. I followed her and behind me Mr. Klok trudged up. He looked tired and I could sympathize. I was tired too. I had no idea what I would say to Mrs. Smit. Sanna, on the other hand, did not seem the least bit intimidated about what was to come. The brown door at the top of the stairs had a small window. I peeked over Sanna's shoulder and saw a hall much like the one we had left on the first floor.

'All right, Sanna. Keep on moving, love. Open the door.'

Mr. Klok was right behind us. Sanna pushed the door open. It creaked ever so slightly. The first door on the right was numbered 239. There was no one in the hall. We walked slowly. My shoes squeaked again and I tried to walk on my toes for a few moments. The doors to most of the rooms were shut. They were all brown doors and they all had a small window, just like the door at the top of the stairs.

The door to room 244 was halfway open. Sanna suddenly stood stock-still.

'I've changed my mind,' she whispered in a very small voice, 'I don't think I want to go in after all, Father.'

Mr. Klok stopped as well.

'You should go in, Sanna,' he said, 'and Nelly will be right there with you, won't you Nelly?'

I nodded. What else could I do?

'I'm sorry I said that about her coat,' Sanna continued her whisper, 'and you could tell her that, couldn't you, Nelly?'

Mr. Klok put his hand on Sanna's shoulder and gave her a small shove towards the open door. 'Go, Sanna,' he said firmly, 'Get it over with.'

Reluctantly Sanna's rubber soles made their way over the threshold. My squeaking shoes followed. Just before I went in Mr. Klok spoke.

'There's a waiting room down the end of the hall. I can see it from here. I'll be there when you're done.'

There were two beds in room 244 with a curtain of sorts hung up between them. The woman in the first bed was lying down flat, her face turned away from us. A cream coloured sheet covered her entire body although her hands were visible on the coverlet. She lay so still, it appeared as if she was not breathing at all. Sanna, after a small look to see if I was still behind her, walked over to the side of the bed. There was a chair and she sat down in it. I stayed at the foot of the bed.

'Hello, Mrs. Smit,' Sanna began, 'I'm sorry that you're in the hospital.'

She paused and studied her fingernails. I noted that they were polished a light red today.

'I guess you might remember me, Sanna Klok.'

I cleared my throat and she glanced at me, slightly irritated.

'I've come to visit because,' Sanna continued, 'because I guess I'm sorry about what I said to you the other day. And because my father made me come. But you know what ...'

Here she sat up straighter and her voice grew louder.

'You know what? Actually I'm not really sorry at all. And why should I lie about that.'

I guess I gasped at this revelation because Sanna looked at me again as if to say, 'Be quiet, and don't interrupt me.'

Mrs. Smit's hand moved and Sanna stood up.

'You know the first time I saw you, which was the first week that we moved here, I began to dislike you. Do you want to know why?'

Mrs. Smit breathing which had been almost imperceptible, became agitated.

'I disliked you because you looked so much like my mother ... like my mother used to look.'

I stared at Sanna.

'My mother was a liar. She lied to me. She promised me that she would stay with me. That she would unlock the door to the cubby-hole that we had made in the wall. That she would never, ever leave me. But you know what. She did leave me. She left me to go to strangers and she never came back.'

I stepped to the opposite side of the bed. Mrs. Smit's rather asthmatic breathing troubled me. Sanna took no note of my moving. She continued to speak.

'And you hit me. You hit me in the face. I know it was because I wouldn't climb into the hole. We could hear the police coming. But wouldn't it have been better for them to take me as well as you? Wouldn't it have been better if both of us had died? And you hit me so hard, so hard that everything went black. And then when I came to ...'

'Sanna!'

My voice was urgent. I interrupted her flow of words and repeated her name again, and she looked at me with a dazed sort of look.

'Sanna, this woman is not Mrs. Smit.'

'She's not?'

Disbelief tinged her voice and for the first time since I knew her, I felt a faint compassion stir in my heart. What if my mother had hit me, had left me somewhere and then had disappeared out of my life forever?

'Well, then who is she?'

'I don't know.'

The woman's eyes were closed and she seemed to be in a heavy, sedated sort of sleep.

'Sanna.'

This time it was not I who spoke but the other woman in the room, the woman who was hidden behind the curtain of the other bed.

'Sanna, come here.'

The voice repeated Sanna's name and Sanna froze in her chair.

'No,' she said softly, 'No, no, no. I will not come.'

'Why not?' the voice asked.

I stood between Sanna and the voice. It is hard to describe exactly how Sanna seemed to shrivel up, how she seemed to be disintegrating before my eyes.

'Because it cannot be. Because I do not believe it. That's why I cannot come.'

The curtain parted slightly and a hand showed through, a small slight hand. The white hospital gown did not quite come up to her wrist and a tiny red birthmark coloured the skin upon the wrist. Slowly, very slowly, Sanna walked over and touched the birthmark.

And I remembered the Thomas story.

Time Like An Ever-Rolling Stream
Bears All Its Sons Away

I am a child and love to walk
In sand, stretching my feet,
Hearing the crying seagulls talk,
Smelling the salt and sweet.
The wind upon my hair and I
Can run among the living. Why
Must dying come to pass?

Warm sand-grains slide between my hands.
The waves embrace the shore.
I love too much! I love this land!
And cannot leave before
I'm pulled away – for I can't stay,
Although this is a golden day,
And I desire more.

The meadow larks and meadow lands
Are fair to look upon,
But they are transient and these hands
Blue-veined, will soon be gone.
Listen! The waves of ebb and tide
Surging past centuries, have cried
That they too pass along.

It makes my heart contract that I
Leave living things; and while
I walk and pace brushing them by,
I covet added miles.
Decades envelop – years must pass –
And break as easily as glass
When thrown upon the floor.

The windows dim, grasshopper I
Have but a mortal name.
My cane, the time allotted by
Creator of my earthly frame.
The silver cord severed from me.
The pitcher shattered helplessly,
And spirit faces God.

'Now all has been heard;
here is the conclusion of the matter:
Fear God and keep His commandments,
for this is the whole duty of man.
For God will bring every deed into judgment,
including every hidden thing,
whether it is good or evil.'
(Ecclesiastes 12:13, 14)

Christine Farenhorst

Meet the Author

Christine Praamsma was born on 10th September, 1948 in a small town in Holland. Her father, a pastor in the Gereformeerde Kerk, accepted a call to Canada in 1958.

Christine began telling stories before she could write. She used to draw pictures on her pillow before she went to sleep at night, relating the stories she drew to her teddy bear.

In 1969 she married her highschool sweetheart, Anco Farenhorst, a veterinarian. By God's grace they became the parents of five children. Grandchildren, as well, have been added to the grains of sand shown so long ago to Abraham.

Christine is also the author of two historical novels: *Wings Like a Dove*, and *A Cup of Cold Water*. As well, she has written several devotionals, other short story volumes, a collection of poetry, and has co-authored two church history text books for children.

A regular columnist for Reformed Perspective as well as a contributing writer for Christian Renewal, her first commitment is to be a godly Christian wife and mother. Her second is to use the talents that God has given her to the best of her ability and to His glory.

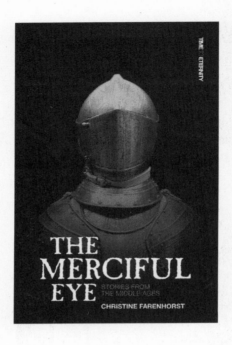

THE MERCIFUL EYE
STORIES FROM THE MIDDLE AGES
CHRISTINE FARENHORST

ISBN: 978-1-84550-562-2

From the depths of history and the dark days of the middle ages we read stories of danger and intrigue but ultimately of faith, hope and love. Jacques hoards his gold, but has yet to find real treasure. A young infant is neglected by his family, but a heavenly father brings him true love.

With these and other stories Christine tells us of tragedy, but also of joy and redemption. These tales are inspired by times past, but ultimately focus on all our futures and the truth of eternity.

HOW GOD STOPPED THE PIRATES
AND OTHER DEVOTIONAL STORIES
JOEL R. BEEKE & DIANA KLEYN

ISBN: 978-1-85792-816-7

As the pirates near the helpless ship they raise their grappling irons and prime their cannons for battle. The captain stands ready to defend his vessel and the lives of the people on board. The missionaries go to their cabins to pray. Can anyone stop these pirates? God can. There are lots of stories in this book. Read about the pirates, a burglar and a Russian servant girl as well as many other stories about the amazing things that missionaries get up to as well as how God can change lives.

Scriptural references are taken from the King James Version of the Bible and the questions are based on this. Suitable for 7-12 year olds.

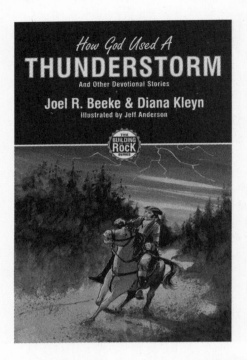

HOW GOD USED A THUNDERSTORM
AND OTHER DEVOTIONAL STORIES
JOEL R. BEEKE & DIANA KLEYN

ISBN: 978-1-85792-815-0

The mountains are dark and looming as the lightening splits across the sky. The forest offers shelter and in the distance the traveller spots a lamp. Rushing towards the door he doesn't realise that someone has planned this journey - there is a woman in the house who needs to hear about her loving Saviour, Jesus Christ. God has sent the traveller to tell her about himself.

There are lots of stories in this book. Read about the thunderstorm, some hidden treasure and a Bible in a suitcase as well as many other stories about how we should live for God and read his word.

The true story of the last days of a young footballer

J H Wilson

Classic Stories

BRIGHT SUNSET
J. H. WILSON
ISBN: 978-1-84550-114-3

This is a true story! William Easton was enthusiastic about everything: School, friends, sports ... especially sports. Physically strong and robust, he was popular among all the other lads in his class at school. On the football field he was known both for his skill and his boundless energy. However, a tragic accident at sixteen years of age confined him to his bed and what everyone thought was just an accident turned out to be something far more serious and life threatening. William's life seems to be in ruins but he discovers, as do others, that in the middle of ruins - you can find treasure. This is the story of a great life given whole-heartedly to God.

HISTORY LIVES: PERIL AND PEACE
CHRONICLES OF THE ANCIENT CHURCH
MINDY AND BRANDON WITHROW
ISBN: 978-1-84550-082-5

Read the stories of Paul, Polycarp, Justin, Origen, Cyprian, Constantine, Athanasius, Ambrose, Augustine, John Chrysostom, Jerome, Patrick, and Benedict. People from the early and ancient church and discover the roots of Christianity. From the apostle Paul to Benedict you can discover how those in the early church still influence church today. Watch in amazement as people from different countries, cultures and times merge together to form the Christian church.

Learn from their mistakes and errors but more importantly learn from their strengths and gifts. Marvel at what God accomplished in such a short space of time.

Written in a modern and relaxed style this is a book that will introduce you to history without the tears and with all the wonder. There are longer chapters interspersed with short factual chapters. Extra features throughout this book look deeper into issues such as persecution; worship; creeds and councils and the formation of the Bible as well as a timeline.

HISTORY LIVES: MONKS AND MYSTICS
CHRONICLES OF THE MEDIEVAL CHURCH
MINDY AND BRANDON WITHROW
ISBN: 978-1-84550-083-2

Read the stories of Gregory the Great, Boniface, Charlemagne, Constantine Methodius, Vladimir, Anselm of Canterbury, Bernard of Clairvaux, Francis of Assisi, Thomas Aquinas, Catherine of Sienna, John Wyclif and John Hus. From Gregory I through to Wyclif and Hus you can discover about the crusades and the spread of Islam as well as the beginnings of universities and the Reformation.

As the church moves on through the centuries its people struggle against persecution and problems from inside and out. Learn from their mistakes and errors but more importantly learn from their amazing strengths and gifts. Marvel at God's wonderful care of his people - the church - the Christian church.

Written in a modern and relaxed style this is a book that will introduce you to history without the tears and with all the wonder. Extra features throughout this book include looking deeper into issues such as Islam; Division; The crusades; the first university; Creeds and Councils and the Renaissance.

CHRISTIAN FOCUS PUBLICATIONS

Christian Christian   CF4K   Mentor
Focus   Heritage

Christian Focus Publications publishes books for adults and children under its four main imprints: Christian Focus, Christian Heritage, CF4K and Mentor. Our books reflect that God's word is reliable and Jesus is the way to know him, and live for ever with him.

Our children's publication list includes a Sunday school curriculum that covers pre-school to early teens; puzzle and activity books. We also publish personal and family devotional titles, biographies and inspirational stories that children will love.

If you are looking for quality Bible teaching for children then we have an excellent range of Bible story and age specific theological books. From pre-school to teenage fiction, we have it covered!

**Find us at our web page:
www.christianfocus.com**

CF4•K
Because you're never
too young to know Jesus